Legends of Glory
AND OTHER STORIES

Other Books by Harry Mark Petrakis

Harry Mark Petrakis

Legends of Glory

AND OTHER STORIES

Southern Illinois University Press
CARBONDALE

"Beauty's Daughter" first appeared in the
Chicago Tribune Sunday Magazine.
"The Birthday," by Harry Mark Petrakis,
copyright © 2002 by Harry Mark Petrakis,
was first published in *New Letters,* volume 69,
number 1, fall 2002. It is printed here with the
permission of *New Letters* and the Curators
of the University of Missouri–Kansas City.
"Christina's Summer" was first published in
Odyssey magazine, July–August 2006.
"The Rousing of Mathon Sarlas" was first published
in *NEO* magazine, spring 2007.
"A Tale of Color" was first published in *MondoGreco,*
issue 6–7, fall 2001–spring 2002.
"The Wisdom of Solon" was first published in
Odyssey magazine, March–April 2004.

Library of Congress Cataloging-in-Publication Data
Petrakis, Harry Mark.
Legends of glory and other stories / Harry Mark Petrakis.
p. cm.
ISBN-13: 978-0-8093-2758-4 (alk. paper)
ISBN-10: 0-8093-2758-9 (alk. paper)
I. Title.
PS3566.E78L44 2007
813'.54—dc22
2006025771

Printed on recycled paper. ♻

The paper used in this publication meets
the minimum requirements of American National
Standard for Information Sciences—Permanence of
Paper for Printed Library Materials, ANSI Z39.48-1992. ∞

For my dearest Diana,
once my young beauty and my old beauty now,
whose love has nourished my work and my life

Contents

For years, each time I entered a certain bakery owned by a sullen-faced Greek man and his lovely, more amiable and pleasant wife, I wondered at the odd pairing and if that public image reflected their private lives. That is all any writer requires, a seed giving birth to reflection that spawns the words to make a story.

Perhaps I have done the real-life baker an injustice. He might in truth be the kindest and most loving of husbands and his wife more shrewish in their home than the persona she reveals in public.

But the reality of their lives does not matter in the story, which establishes a reality of its own. If there is anything truer than truth, it is legend.

Beauty's Daughter

MY MOTHER, WHO BORE THE NAME OF APHRODITE, the Greek goddess of beauty, was also a very beautiful woman. As a child, I remember watching her sitting before her mirror brushing her long black hair. When the brush in her hand descended from the crown to the nape, her hair glistened with a soft, alluring sparkle. Within the cascade of her hair, her face was a pale, smooth oval graced with great dark eyes. In some ways I resembled my mother, but I also had the physical attributes of my father that made me look more coarse and common.

My mother and father's marriage had been arranged by their families. Their parents had been close friends. The families had agreed early that my mother would be married to Nicholas, who was near her own age. But Nicholas was killed in an auto accident when he was nineteen. The grieving families still wished to be bonded by marriage, and they arranged for my mother to wed Nicholas's older brother, Aristides, who was then thirty-four, ten years older than my mother.

I have only seen photographs of the young man who was to have married my mother and who might have become my father. He was handsome, but beyond his physical attributes, there was a lightness and laughter in his face and eyes totally alien to anything I ever saw in the face of my father.

I

My earliest memories of my father were those of a morose, brooding man. He rarely laughed and seemed somehow to darken any room or conversation he entered. In contrast, my mother was lighthearted and cheerful, quick to laugh and eager to praise. In any gathering of people, men and women were drawn to her, while my father often sat alone in some corner.

My parents owned a small bakery on Halsted Street, one among a number of other Greek stores, and we lived in an apartment above the store. Our bakery had several glass counters that held the trays of assorted pastries. (My task from childhood was to keep the glass of the counters sparkling clean.) There were also two small tables for patrons to sit and have a cup of coffee with their sweets.

The kitchen where we baked our pastries was always scented with the fragrance of flour, butter, and honey. As a child I would sit on a high stool and watch my parents baking. Even during the coldest days of winter, the kitchen was warm and nested. My parents would knead the dough and cut the pastry filo, then put the raw sweets onto the trays and slip them into the ovens. When the trays were removed from the ovens, the pastries were golden brown. My mother dipped them into honey or sprinkled powdered sugar across the crisp crust.

In all their labors together, my parents never seemed in any harmony of spirit. My mother worked buoyantly, smiling at me from time to time, letting me taste a corner of some freshly baked pastry even as my father grumbled that she was fostering in me an addiction for sweets. But my greatest pleasure in the kitchen wasn't to taste the pastries; it was simply to watch my mother. I loved to look at her, marveling even then at her beauty, which was enhanced by the traces of flour and butter like tiny adornments on her cheeks that accentuated the glow of her dark eyes.

My father worked hard but never seemed to take any joy in his labor. He rarely spoke except to hiss some complaint to my mother about something she was doing. Nothing she did appeared to please him. His rebukes were petty and constant. But my mother took them all in good humor, never challenging him, never allowing his comments to provoke a fight.

By the time I was fourteen, helping in the baking myself, I was more bothered by my father's endless criticism than my mother was. On a few occasions I tried to defend her, and then my father would include me in his reprimand.

"Like mother, like daughter," he snapped. "If you model yourself after her, you will never do anything right."

I felt an urge to tell my father how much I wanted to be like my mother, but my mother's face warned me not to defy him. Afterward, when he had departed on some errand, she sought to justify his ill temper.

"Your father works very hard, Despina," she said. "He has built a good business here and is respected as being fair by our patrons and by the other storekeepers. We are warm and have all we want to eat. If he is cross sometimes, it is because there are things that trouble him."

I did not learn until my sophomore year in high school that what troubled my father was that my mother had not been able to give him a son. Within a year after I had been born, she developed some infection in her female organs that left her sterile and unable to conceive any more children.

I told my mother that I had heard my father voice his grievance to an acquaintance who had come into the bakery when he did not know I was in the kitchen. She sought to reassure me that his desire for a son did not mean he did not love me. She told me it was natural for any man to want a son who would carry on his name.

"I will keep his name, Mama," I said.

"You will always have his name my darling," my mother said, "but when you marry, you will also assume your husband's name."

"Then I will never marry," I said earnestly. "That way I will always have our name and he will not need to be unhappy because he does not have a son."

In my conversations with my mother, I only referred to my father as "he." In speaking to him, I never used "Papa" or "Father" but used the pronoun "you"—"Do you want me to do this?" "Will you let me do that?"

My father never struck my mother, and I was grateful to him for that. But as I grew into my teen years, I understood that his blows were damaging, emotional ones. As hard as my mother sought to please him and avoid incurring his displeasure, he still complained about her constantly. Whether it was the way she baked, or the length of time it took her to wait on a customer, or the dress she chose to wear to church, or the time she took in being kind to others, his censure and disapproval were relentless. The result was a certain weariness that pervaded the way my mother moved and spoke and a diminishment of pleasure in her work and in her life.

When I entered my senior year in high school, my days were occupied with schoolwork and other activities, and I spent less time in the bakery. But I never forgot my parents for very long. As I sat with a group of girls listening to their chatter, I thought of my mother and father working in silence in the shop. When I was with them, my conversation seemed to lighten my mother's burden. Not being there with her seemed almost a betrayal.

When it was time for my high school senior prom, my mother wanted me to have a fine new dress. She had told me on more than one occasion that I was a pretty girl, and she took time and pleasure in helping me select my clothing. My father invariably complained about the cost, counting such expenditures "frivolous and unnecessary."

The dress my mother helped me select was more expensive than anything we had ever bought before. I was worried that my father would be angry with her, but my mother reassured me. As I had expected, though, my father criticized the cost and insisted, "The dress goes back to the thief who sold it to you!"

For the first time, my mother challenged him. She told him quietly but with a vein of firmness in her voice that she worked in the bakery as long and as hard as he did and that whatever profit they made was hers as well. If she chose to spend some of it on a dress for me, she had that right. My father gave in, grumbling and resentful, and we kept the dress. But the night of the prom was shadowed for me by the memory of his complaints. Afterward, I put the dress away in a storage bag in the back of my closet.

Among the other Greek stores on the street where our bakery was located was a grocery run by two brothers, Kostas and Manolis Sorvonis. They were from the same town in Greece my grandparents had come from. Kostas was the older brother and was married, with two children. Manolis was still single and about my mother's age. He was rather short in stature and not a very handsome man, but he had a laughing, carefree demeanor that made his presence heartwarming in the somber confines of our shop. After Manolis left the bakery, a certain cheerfulness and zest departed with him.

The Sorvonis brothers would buy trays of pastries from us and, from time to time, would have a cup of coffee in our shop with my father while discussing business relating to the street. But Manolis began coming alone into the store more frequently, lingering over a cup of coffee, chatting with my mother. He seemed to know when my father was away and would choose that time to come to our store. My mother and I were both sparked by his presence, and after he left I noticed that my mother returned to work with a renewed animation, a faint flush crimsoning her cheeks.

I think I began to love Manolis the summer after I graduated from high school. He brought me a small gift for my graduation, a music box on which a tiny slender dancer twirled while a haunting melody played. I treasured the music box and often played it a number of times before going to sleep.

Manolis was also a wonderful storyteller. He would relate stories such as that of Jason and the Argonauts so vividly that he might have been one of the shipwrecked members of that valiant crew who sailed with the hero for the Golden Fleece. His stories became so alive for me that at night, in my dreams, I heard the rough voices and laughter of those men bound for glory and adventure.

Manolis also spoke of the great heroines of legend, of Calypso, Nausicaä, and Penelope, who waited ten years for the return of her beloved Odysseus. He told us that all the heroines were really one woman who could be different at various times—shy and timid, promiscuous, loving and beloved.

I understood that in the eyes of Manolis, I remained little more than a child. He was always pleasant and affectionate with me because that was his nature. But in the same way that I found my own feelings for him sharpened, I felt his intensity directed toward my mother. When she waited on a customer, he watched her with a look of reverence on his face. When she brought him another cup of coffee or bent closer to him to give him another sweet, her nearness seemed to make him tremble. As I loved Manolis, I understood that he loved my mother.

I could not be with them every time they were together, so I had no way of knowing for sure how my mother responded to him. But in his presence she seemed to emanate a vibrancy and heightened beauty. She took longer to dress in the morning, longer to brush her hair. She was more careful that the smock she wore was freshly laundered.

I understood the delight Manolis must have felt looking upon my mother's loveliness. But then I could not believe that any man, old or young, existed anywhere on earth who would not love my mother.

One day when the three of us were laughing together, Manolis quoted the lines from a poem he said was written by a great English poet, Lord Byron. He looked at my mother as he spoke the lines:

"There be none of Beauty's daughters
With a magic like thee,
And like music on the waters
Is thy sweet voice to me."

When Manolis had finished, I saw my mother's face, warmed and tender, as if she had just been caressed.

My father noticed that Manolis was spending an inordinate amount of time in the bakery. He complained to my mother that she need not continue a conversation with the grocer after she had served him. He made caustic references to Manolis as indolent and lazy, leaving his brother alone to do all the work.

There was a night when my father was at a meeting of his lodge brothers. Manolis had been with us for several hours, and at closing time, after we locked the door, I left him with my mother in the kitchen while I cleaned the remaining crumbs from the trays. While I worked in the front, their laughter carried to me in waves of mirth.

At some point, I was conscious of a silence in the kitchen. I waited for their voices to resume, but the stillness continued. At the same time, I sensed a curious alteration of emotion in the constricted confines of the store. I was so close to my mother's heart that I suddenly felt my own heart accelerate as if it were beating with hers. A tingling excitement possessed me, and I wanted to go into the kitchen to see what was happening, but I did not dare move or make a sound.

Then, in the tense, highly strung silence, I heard my mother sigh. It was as if she had been holding her breath and suddenly released it. I did not know for sure whether Manolis had kissed her, but I knew that for the first time there had been some physical intimacy between them.

My own feelings were tangled. I felt jealous of my mother and resentful that Manolis would choose her to love instead of me. But an emotion stronger than jealousy was joy that Manolis had found my mother so beautiful that he wished to touch her. From that night on, Manolis did not appear as often in the store. My father commented on his absence by saying, "Good riddance to the loafer." But I did not believe that his absence meant he was no longer interested in my mother. I believed both of them understood the danger of revealing their feelings in the presence of each other. I think they were content to wait.

Early in August of that year, my father received word that his sister, Froso, had died in Cleveland. They had never been close, but my father felt obligated to go to the funeral. My mother thought we should go with him, but he did not wish to close the store. He would be gone for only two days, so he left us to look after the business.

That first night after my father had left, while my mother and I ate supper, I noticed a restlessness about her. She walked from room to room, her shadow sweeping fitfully along the walls. Finally she said she was going to go downstairs to roll some dough. I suggested going with her, but she told me she wanted me to sleep well because the following day would be a busy one without my father to help in the store.

After my mother had left the apartment, I washed and dried the dishes. I tried to read a little, and then I got ready for bed. I had a feeling then that my mother had left the bakery. I could have gone downstairs to see for myself, but I did not leave the apartment.

When it came time for me to put on my nightgown, I slipped naked into my bed. Whether it was my nakedness or because I suspected that my mother was with Manolis, in the span of that night I felt my own body glowing and alive. As the time passed and my mother did not return, I understood that she was with Manolis. Knowing suddenly that the two of them were making love transferred a softness and sensitivity to my own flesh.

In some uncertain hour of the night, I heard my mother return, though she moved quietly through the rooms in order not to wake me. I traced her passage through the hallway and heard her pause, listening outside my door. I thought surely she must hear the frantic beating of my heart. Then she moved on into the bathroom, with the faint sound of the running water, and then she entered her bedroom. I imagined her slipping into bed, perhaps weary but also exultant with the feeling of love. I entered into her body then, my love for her allowing me to feel what she was feeling, her passion extending through the walls of my room to me.

When the first glimmerings of dawn appeared around the perimeter of my shade, I rose and slipped into my nightgown. Before returning to bed, I pushed the shade aside and saw the earth in that moment as I had never seen it before. It was as if the night had not yet relinquished its power, as if the light had not yet gained dominance. In that ancient moment of confrontation between light and dark, for the first time I understood the word "love." I repeated the single syllable several times, felt it like a caress upon my tongue. Then I climbed into bed and slept.

In the weeks that followed that night, I marked the changes in my mother. She seemed to move with an enhanced grace and a renewed sense of purpose.

My father also saw the changes in her, and it bewildered and frightened him, as if he sensed she was no longer within the dominion of his influence. I trembled in apprehension of what he might do if he found out. Although he had never struck my mother before, I wondered if he would strike her then.

There was a day near the end of that August, a day when the city drifted within a web of moisture and heat. I came home from the library to find the bakery closed several hours before the usual closing time. A strange fear suddenly pervaded my body, and I went around to the back door leading up to our apartment and quietly let myself in.

As I slowly climbed the stairs, I heard the voices of my father and my mother, and with a surge of terror, I heard the name of Manolis. I knew then that my father had learned about my mother and her lover. I waited for the unleashing of his rage, but when I came closer to the kitchen door, I heard his voice as I had never heard it before—weeping, vulnerable, stricken. I did not know my father could cry that way: a cascade of tears seemed to be welling up from somewhere deep within his body. I also heard him pleading with my mother not to leave him, assuring her of his love, asking her forgiveness for all his slights, imploring her not to stop loving him.

I felt as if I were watching my father and mother in their nakedness, and I turned away and quietly went back down the stairs. I walked to the candle store on the corner and visited for almost an hour with Mrs. Lentzos. When I returned home, my heart beating at the turmoil and shambles I might find there, it was as if nothing had happened. The table in the dining room was set for dinner. My mother was cooking in the kitchen. My father sat in his armchair reading his Greek paper. But even when we sat down to eat our dinner, each of us putting food into our mouths as we had done so many times before, I felt that a change had come into our lives and that nothing again would ever be the same.

Each day that passed, I waited for my mother to run away with Manolis. I was heartsick because I might lose her, but in a vengeful, vindictive way, I wanted that to happen so that my father would be punished.

But Manolis was the one who left, not my mother, and he left alone, moving to another city. I did not know what words or decisions had transpired between the two of them, but I think that when Manolis understood that my mother would not leave my father, he could no longer bear to be near her, to continue to desire her.

For a little while I was possessed by many reckless and brazen thoughts. Since my mother had rejected Manolis, I considered pursuing him for myself. But I realized how foolhardy that would be, a betrayal of my mother's decision and a violation of her love. However hard it was for me to lose Manolis, it was a more difficult severance of flesh and spirit for her.

In the months that followed the departure of Manolis, my mother, father, and I passed the cycle of our lives as we had lived it before. Yet it was different. My mother had gained a power that my father mutely acknowledged. It was as if all his force had fled and found a place in her body. I did not believe they found love again, but they had fashioned a kind of harmony and tranquillity. My mother had made her choice, and for that my father was grateful, and he became kinder to her and more considerate of her than he had ever been before.

In the fall of that year I left for college in another state. My mother no longer needed me, and I was ready to leave. By that time, I understood more clearly the significance of what had taken place. As a witness to my mother's brief moment of passion and happiness, I gained an understanding of what love should be like. When I enter the world for myself, that is the kind of love I will seek, and I will not settle for less. My mother's joy was brief, but her legacy to me will be lasting, a legacy that allows me to understand, for as long as I live, the rapture that can exist in life when one has found one's love.

I once heard a mentally myopic talk show host ask the octogenarian writer Henry Miller whether he ever thought of death. Miller looked at the clod with a kind of pity and said quietly, "All the time."

As I've aged myself, I don't think of death all the time, but it does come into my head fairly often—not so much death but the process by which it will signal its arrival. Will it be sudden, or will it come after a lingering illness? I once feared I wouldn't live long enough, and now I fear I may live too long.

Mostly, my fear is the fear many people have: the emotional and physical decline that the years can bring. At the same time, there is a certain feeling of reassurance and solace that comes of believing that death constitutes part of the harmony that makes up life. As another poet, whose name now I cannot recall, has written, "For a wise man a single lifetime should be enough, since a stupid man wouldn't know what to do with eternity anyway."

Meanwhile, with each birthday that makes us older, one must draw gratefully upon the bounty that time and experience bring to us. Age doesn't always make us wiser, but it should provide us with a greater understanding of the earth with its mirrors, its marvels, and its guile, while living and attempting the precarious and elusive task of adjusting to our own flaws should make us more tolerant of the flaws of others.

The Birthday

WHEN ANDREAS WOKE THAT MORNING OF HIS BIRTHDAY, he opened his eyes reluctantly to the morning sun rimming the shade of his window. He stared at his bureau, at the books on the end table, at the painting of Andrew Wyeth's model, Helga, on the wall. Everything appeared the same. The only difference is that I am seventy-five, he thought, three-quarters of a century old, a meager five years away from eighty. If I last that long.

He rose from his bed, feeling a more pervasive stiffness in his joints than he had felt the morning before. That is because I am one year older, he thought gloomily.

In the bathroom he stared at his face in the vanity mirror, a reflection he had been confronting all his life. Never even in his youth a handsome face, but he hoped a face reflecting some character.

He tried to appraise his visage as it might be viewed by a stranger. Deep-set eyes, one lid drooping, cheeks furrowed, gray hair and receding hairline, large ears, prominent jaw.

In similar fashion, he assessed his faculties. He had a slight myopia in his eyes with a dryness that required drops. His hearing, sense of taste, and sense of smell were good. He was about ten pounds over-weight but remained active by cycling and swimming. His general health was positive without any known heart or cancer problems. His prostate, that jewel of a man's ascending years, was enlarged (requiring nocturnal journeys to the bathroom) but benign.

He paused with his razor poised and shrugged. When all is said and done, he thought, I should be thankful to have lasted this long without a major affliction. Yet the chronology was inescapable. Perhaps seventy-five was a warning to get ready for what no one can ever be ready for.

After shaving, he slipped into his bathrobe and walked quietly down the hallway past the room where his wife, Dessie, was still asleep. They had slept in the same bed for many years, but as their sleep patterns grew more erratic, they found it more comfortable to sleep in separate bedrooms. Sometimes, on cold winter nights or on those less frequent times when desire sparked them, they shared the double bed.

He usually rose about an hour before his wife. That gave him a chance to make the coffee (Dessie tended to brew it too strong) and to squeeze some oranges. By the time he had poured the glasses of juice and divided their assorted vitamin tablets, Dessie entered the kitchen in her white terrycloth robe and bent to give him a gentle kiss.

"Happy birthday, my darling."

"I know I'll be reminded of my age many times today."

"Don't be like Tony," Dessie said, referring to a close friend. "Mention his birthday and he sulks for days. You're alert and still writing well seven years after you retired from the paper. You have a loving, although aging, wife, loving children, and loving grand-children. That's a great deal."

He had to agree.

They ate a light breakfast of English muffins, cheese, and coffee. Andreas read the paper while Dessie turned on the small-screen

TV above the refrigerator to watch the morning news. She kept the volume low because she knew he preferred the silence.

But the news was the same in both mediums. The flight and murder of refugees in Kosovo, another bombing in Northern Ireland, Saddam Hussein rejecting the arms inspectors. Within their own city of Chicago, several robberies, the wrangling of politicians, a rape in Lincoln Park. He thought sometimes that his eldest son, Nick, in Colorado, was right when he suggested starting one's day in meditation.

On this morning of his birthday, under the pretext of reading his paper, he found himself studying Dessie, who was intent on the TV screen, appraising her as he had earlier evaluated himself.

She was a year younger than he was and in general good health as well. While she also had added weight over the years, her figure was still comely. Her thick, long hair, which had once been raven-black, was now streaked with gray and had lost its youthful luster. Beneath her large dark eyes a web of tiny wrinkles pinched at her flesh. Sometimes it seemed to him she looked her years, but when she smiled or laughed, he recaptured glimpses of the lovely young girl she had been when they first married. Because of her beauty, he found the signs of her aging more disheartening than his own.

They had been married fifty years. That union had provided many joyful and rewarding interludes as well as some small and large failures and a few times of anguish. Early in their marriage they suffered the death of their first child, Anthony. The boy had been born with a congenital heart defect that took his life when he was six months old. Both Andreas and Dessie grieved, but her anguish sent her into a long, terrible depression so pervasive that for a while it seemed she might have to be hospitalized. Finally, a sensitive and understanding psychiatrist was able to convince her that she was not responsible for the loss of the baby. Yet the death inflicted a wound in Dessie from which she had never really recovered. Many years later, even after the birth of their other children, when Andreas saw her sitting alone, staring mutely at some ghost only she could see, he knew she was thinking of the lost baby.

She hadn't been responsible for the baby's death, but Andreas was fully responsible for another crisis in their lives when, for a period of several years, he drank too much and caroused with other young reporters from the paper. A time came when he could not conceal his derelictions from Dessie. Yet, in spite of the pain he caused her, she had found the tolerance and strength to forgive his neglect and infidelities. What made her forgiveness more formidable was that he wasn't sure he would have been able to forgive her if their flaws had been reversed.

She caught him staring at her.

"What are you thinking about?" she asked.

"I was just figuring that putting our ages together, we have lived almost 150 years. That number has a biblical ring to it."

"Everybody in the Bible lived a long time," she smiled. "That was without Medicare, too."

He finished his breakfast and rose to shower and dress.

"What are your plans today?" Dessie asked.

"I'll put in my usual hours at the library and then go over to Karoll's studio for a while. Shall I ask him and Sarah to join us for the party tonight?"

"If you'd like to," Dessie said. "It will just be the kids and us. If they want to come, I'm sure there'll be enough food for two more."

"We should have planned to go to a restaurant," he said. "You'll be celebrating my birthday by cooking all afternoon."

"I don't mind. Jerry and Pam will be bringing appetizers and the cake. You know it's hard eating in a restaurant with the children. We'll all enjoy the evening more here at home."

Before he left the house he kissed Dessie once more, and she told him to be careful. The routine was identical to the one they shared each morning.

He drove out of the garage of their house on the northwest side of the city into the traffic on Devon. He rolled down his window to inhale the balmy scents of the June day. The month of his birth was often a lovely bridge between spring and the heat of midsummer. He was suddenly grateful that he had not been born in winter.

Inside the library he took his usual place at one of the tables in the research section. He relocated the reference books on Chicago gangsters he had been using to help him with his biography of Johnny Torreo, the mastermind behind Al Capone. Andreas had been working on the book for almost two years and hoped to have it completed within six months to fulfill the publishing contract he had signed. He had written two earlier books on his newspaper days since he retired from the paper.

His daily routine was to work four or five hours, but that morning he couldn't concentrate. He rose restlessly from the table to wander along the stacks. In one of the alcove reading chairs, a young man sat intently over a book.

The man's preoccupation recalled for Andreas how he had always loved libraries and the bounty of books they contained. As a youth he had played hooky from school so he could spend his hours reading in the library.

He remembered his awe before the thousands of volumes that lined the shelves. He had favored new books that had not yet been eroded and worn by many hands. He'd stroke the bindings, admire the jacket art. Sometimes he raised the open book to his nostrils and inhaled the smell that rose from new paper and fresh ink. He now did this warily, since a librarian had once seen him performing that ritual and had accused him of some aberration.

He no longer spent hours reading as he had once done. There were the problems with his eyes and also the pressures of his days that left him with little time. Or was that simply an excuse for a mental laziness that came with age?

After a fruitless morning, he gathered his papers at about one o'clock and left the library. He walked to a nearby Chinese restaurant and ordered shrimp chow mein to take out. Then he drove a few miles north to the house on Howard Street where his friends Karoll and Sarah Menchoff lived.

He parked and walked around the house to the large garage Karoll had converted into a studio. He heard the sound of the chisel striking wood as he knocked. Karoll's hoarse voice answered.

Andreas entered the large studio that was sparsely furnished except for a cot in the corner. The walls held an assortment of charcoal-and-ink sketches of heads and torsos. A half-dozen completed wood sculptures perched on small tables. There was a winged Icarus, the head of a child, and a number of male and female figures, solitary or coupled in supple, flowing forms.

In the midst of this gallery, Karoll worked at a long table. A slab of still, formless wood stood on its surface, chips and shavings cluttered around the base.

"I didn't expect to see you today," Karoll said. The sculptor's voice was imbued with the heavy middle-European accent of his homeland, Russia. "I thought you'd have more important things to do on your birthday."

"Nothing could be more meaningful than a chow mein lunch with you," Andreas said.

"You're a good, loyal friend," Karoll smiled.

He was ten years older than Andreas, a former newspaper photographer who at the age of seventy gave up photography and moved to sculpture because he wanted his hands and not a machine creating his art. He had chosen to work in wood, beginning with sections of the trunks of trees that his artistry refined into stunning sculptures. For the last few years he had been working on a series of poses from the *Kama Sutra,* the manual on Hindu lovemaking. He fashioned male and female figures emerging out of the wood in marvelous renderings of sensuality and beauty.

"Sit down and I'll get beers from the cooler," Karoll said. The sculptor was shorter than average height with thick steel-gray hair and a striking hawk-face above a lean and wiry body. In marked contrast to his meager-fleshed frame, he had great, strong hands with massive fingers and thumbs almost as thick as a man's wrist. His fingers and palms were also scarred with cuts and marred with calluses.

Karoll bent slowly and painfully to lift the beers from the cooler in the corner. The years of hammering and chiseling at the hard wood had deteriorated the joints of his shoulders and arms so that he moved and worked with constant pain. He opened the beers as Andreas unpackaged the chow mein.

"How old are you today?" Karoll asked.

"Seventy-five," Andreas said. "When I say it, I feel like Methuselah."

"Wait till you get to be eighty-five like me."

"Do I get a medal if I survive that long?"

"You'll win what I have," Karoll grunted. "Sallow complexion, smell like a goat, flat-footed, shaky legs, organs groaning, joints creaking, body fossilized."

He recited the litany of disaster in a calm, expressionless voice.

"I knew you'd be the one to cheer me up."

"Cheering up is for children and expectant mothers," Karoll said. He took another forkful of the chow mein, followed by a long swallow of beer. He rose to return to his bench.

"If I stop for too long I get stiff," he said.

He picked up his chisel and hammer and resumed chipping at the wood.

Andreas finished eating and sat watching the sculptor at work. It seemed to him an inordinately slow and laborious process, each blow of the chisel and hammer dislodging only the tiniest particle of wood. Chip by chip, the particles accumulated around the trunk and base of the table.

"What will this finished piece be?" Andreas asked.

"A male and female figure."

"Making love?"

"I'm not sure," Karoll said. "As they begin to emerge from the wood, they will enlighten me as to who they are and what they wish to do. The woman may be a virgin or a harlot, the man a satyr or a saint."

Andreas felt Karoll was a great artist whose work one day would be eagerly bought by collectors. Yet in all their conversations, the sculptor seemed oblivious to any considerations of fortune or fame.

"Did you work on your book today?" Karoll asked. His words were punctuated by the sound of the chisel.

"I tried but couldn't really concentrate."

"Nothing, even a birthday, should stand in the way of your working daily," Karoll said. "To work well as you age is to combat one of the worst afflictions of aging, which is giving up, slumped in front of the boob box, your arteries hardening while you wait to die."

"That certainly doesn't apply to you," Andreas said. "I admire your discipline and wish I had it."

"Struggle to develop it!" Karoll spoke with intensity. "Then for whatever time you're still given on earth, you may find a way to make your life not just endurable but also worthy of celebration."

"How does one achieve that?"

"Work! Work!" Karoll said. "Work and think! Don't live thoughtlessly. Try to rid yourself of fear and hope. That is the only way to live truly free." He paused. "Remember Yeats's poem 'Sailing to Byzantium'? Remember the line that says 'And therefore I have sailed the seas and come / To the holy city of Byzantium'?"

"What did Byzantium mean to Yeats?"

"It could mean many things to different people," Karoll said. "For me it means that harmony at the core of the earth itself and our role in it. The one great story each of us lives is our search to find our place in the drama."

"What about you? Have you discovered that harmony?"

"I catch glimpses of it from time to time," Karoll said. "Then I fall back into my ego and my mortal carcass. Someday, somehow, I may be able to retain the vision for good."

Karoll turned back to his work. Andreas sat unmoving for almost an hour, marveling at how all the pain and stiffness in Karoll's body was being sublimated into his creation. In the corners of the studio, the consummate sculptures watched in silent approval.

Karoll finally put down his tools.

"I have to stop now," he said wearily. He motioned toward the cot. "I need to stretch out for a little while."

Andreas rose to leave.

"Do you want to bring Sarah to my birthday party this evening?" he asked. "It will just be our kids and their children. You know we would all love to have you. I'll even absolve you from having to bring me a present."

"Your offer's tempting, my friend," Karoll said. "But I'm very tired now, and I'll be even more tired tonight," he smiled. "But I'll think good thoughts for you."

"And I'll keep good thoughts for you," Andreas said. "You are traveling a road that as long as I stay alive I also hope to travel. So I can learn from you."

"Don't learn too much from me." Karoll frowned. "The roads are different, and each man must make his own journey."

He reached out slowly and embraced Andreas with trembling arms, his body emitting smells of wood, weariness, and sweat.

When Andreas left Karoll's studio, he got into his car and on a sudden impulse drove across the city to the South Side cemetery where his father and mother were buried. He passed between the iron gates and the sign that read "Hours: 8 A.M. to 8 P.M." and parked at the small greenhouse to buy fresh flowers. He got back in his car and drove deeper into the fields embedded with monuments and markers.

He parked on the road below his family graves and walked up the slope toward a brown granite cross. The three graves were in the section belonging to the South Side Greek church where he had grown up. All the names on the gravestones around his family's graves he recognized as parishioners in the church. He felt a certain consolation because his loved ones lay in the midst of friends.

He placed flowers on the graves of his father and mother and also beside his son's small headstone. He would have been the oldest of his and Dessie's children, and for a moment Andreas wondered what manner of man he would have been if he had lived.

Beside the three graves, two empty sites remained that Andreas had set aside for Dessie and himself.

In the silence of the cemetery, his mother's voice rose to him through the flowers. He couldn't make out her words, but as he had so often heard when he was both child and adult, her tone was sharp with a reprimand for some transgression he had done.

He stood staring down at the graves, remembering a time when his parents had been guardians of his brother, his sister, and himself. As a child when he woke from a frightening dream, one or the other would come to comfort him. He believed for a while that they did not actually sleep but remained awake like sentries to protect him against the terrors of the night. As he grew older, he came to understand their mortality.

His father had owned a small restaurant that he operated with very little help for almost thirty years, wrenching a living for his family only by his arduous and unremitting labor. His wife had helped him by cooking for the patrons in the old kitchen with the ancient stove and often waited on customers, as well. Even before they had graduated from elementary school, Andreas and his brother and sister were conscripted into service, washing dishes, sweeping the floor, and polishing the pie case and counters. None of them enjoyed the work, but Andreas loathed everything about the place: the oppressive odors of dishwater and grease, the carping of often disgruntled patrons. He sought every means to avoid working there, in terror of falling into the trap that had imprisoned his father, having to depend upon the restaurant as a livelihood.

The incessant labor and the endless hours finally killed his father. A customer found him one morning on the floor in the kitchen not long after he had opened the restaurant. His beleaguered heart had finally given up.

His mother, who lived an additional twenty years after his father's death, was left almost penniless. But she was a strong, resourceful woman who worked diligently at cooking in other restaurants and, in the evenings, sewed dresses for affluent parishioners. Through their high school years, each of her children also worked at jobs after school to help meet the expenses of the family.

Andreas's brother and sister married and left to live in other parts of the country. Andreas remained at home with his mother. When he and Dessie married, they rented a house with an extra bedroom so his mother could move in with them. None of them expected his mother would live with them for fifteen more years, through the purchase of several houses and the birth of several children. Those were difficult years. Because of her dominant nature, she could not refrain from offering advice whether it was wanted or not. She was that way with Dessie and with their children, nagging them about the things she felt they should be doing. Yet she was also a loving and devout grandmother who helped spoil the children.

In the winter of her eighty-fourth year, his mother became ill with flu that developed into a severe pneumonia. After she'd spent several weeks in the hospital, her doctor advised a recovery period in a nursing facility to regain her strength. For the following two months, Andreas and Dessie were alone for the first time in fifteen years. When the doctor said they could bring his mother home, Andreas made the painful decision to leave her in the facility. That wasn't an arbitrary choice: her mobility had greatly diminished and he and Dessie could no longer provide the care she needed.

His mother never forgave him for not bringing her home, and each time he visited her in the bleak confines of the facility, he felt the lash of her brooding temper and her condemnation at what she believed to be his betrayal. That resentment prevailed until, at the beginning of her fifth year in the facility, trying to climb past the guardrails on her bed, she fell. She lived in a coma for two days while Dessie and he sat on either side of her bed, holding her hands. A moment came when her body trembled, her lips exhaled a sudden short current of air, and she died.

A slight wind rose and rustled the cemetery trees, fluttering the petals of the flowers he had laid on the graves. He whispered a small prayer then, on this day of his birthday, asking forgiveness once again from his parents for his derelictions and flaws.

Do all sons and daughters, no matter how old they become, he thought sadly, feel sorrow and remorse when they stand beside their parents' graves? Is it in the nature of mortals that we forsake those who came before? Will that be the legacy Dessie and I will inherit from our own children, as well?

But the silent cemetery with the graves of the dead adorned by fresh or withered flowers could provide no answer. After a while, he left.

Back at home that evening, he helped Dessie cut up the tomatoes and lettuce for the salad. She told him her mother and brother had called from Akron for his birthday. His brother had also called from California and his sister from Missouri. Their son Nick had called from Colorado and would phone again.

In the warm kitchen, Dessie's face was flushed, and several strands of hair had fallen across her cheek. She had been cooking all afternoon, and she seemed to him to look weary and worn, an aging woman pushing herself to do what she could no longer accomplish with ease. He felt a surge of love and compassion for her.

Then because they had lived together so long that they often sensed one another's emotions and thoughts, she looked at him, as if understanding what he had been thinking. She shook her head in rueful agreement with his somber assessment, and then she laughed. The laughter's warmth peeled years from her face.

The front doorbell rang, and he went to answer. His two-year-old grandson, Tommy, leaped in to hug him around the legs. He lifted his grandson to kiss him, savoring the glowing beauty of the child's face. His son Jerry and his wife, Pam, also embraced him and wished him happy birthday.

Within a few minutes his daughter, Artemis, arrived with her husband, Eric, and their five-year-old daughter, Melissa. His granddaughter carried cards and presents for Andreas, and he hugged and kissed her as well.

Jerry was a teacher at a downtown college, and his wife worked as a nurse. Artemis worked in public relations for an accounting firm, and her husband was an attorney. One family lived in Evanston and the other in Des Plaines, so they were able to get together with Andreas and Dessie fairly often for barbecues in summer, dinners in winter, and various celebrations throughout the year.

That evening resembled so many other pleasant ones the family had spent together, replete with laughter, quick and humorous sallies, and Dessie's savory food. The grandchildren raced around, unleashing bedlam, yet with a familiarity and jubilation that Andreas enjoyed.

With the heightened perception the day had brought him, he appraised his family with satisfaction. They were bright, attractive, and sensible young people. Their son and daughter had married well, and their spouses were also devoted to Dessie and to him. He had no grievance with any of his family except a regret that their son Nick had been married and divorced.

When it came time for the birthday cake, his grandchildren gathered beside him, eager to join him in blowing out the candles. Dessie turned off the lights, and his daughter carried in the cake.

"You cheated, Mom," Jerry said. "There aren't seventy-five candles on that cake."

"The baker told me they couldn't bake a cake that large," Dessie said, and everyone laughed.

Artemis placed the cake on the table before Andreas. Tommy and Melissa leaned forward, their noses almost touching the frosting. They all sang "Happy Birthday" in a discordant clamor of voices. Tommy strained forward to blow before the singing had been completed. Melissa protested being left out, and the candles were lit a second time. The children blew in unison and clapped when the candles were extinguished.

"Speech, Papa," Artemis said.

For a moment, Andreas considered speaking of the things he and

Karoll had discussed earlier in the day, how a man should struggle to make aging worthy of celebration and strive to dispel hope and fear so he might live free. Then he looked at their young faces and knew such thoughts could be shared only with other old men. He drew a deep breath.

"Thank you for celebrating this milestone birthday with me," Andreas said. "And thank your mother for all her labor in preparing this savory dinner. Like a great athlete, she may have lost a step or two in the kitchen, but she's still a champion. All of you here, especially Tommy and Melissa, but all of you and your mother will be my birthday presents for as long as we share birthdays together."

Everyone clapped. Andreas looked at Dessie, who had tears in her eyes. She blew him a silent kiss.

Later, when the family had gone, the house silent once again, he went to help Dessie in the kitchen.

"There's very little to do," she said. "Artemis and Pam are great at cleaning up, and Jerry did the pots. I'm just putting what's left of the food away. By the time you've showered, I'll be up."

He started from the kitchen. She called him back.

"Did you have a good time tonight, honey?" she asked. "You seemed quiet . . . maybe a little sad."

"Seventy-five has made me think back over my life" Andreas said. "There are so many things to remember."

"I know," Dessie sighed. She stared at him with concern. "Let's sleep together tonight. Okay?"

"That's fine." he said.

"I just think we should be together for the wind-up of your birthday."

The beam of moonlight coming in the front windows of the room illuminated portions of their bed. From the street below came the bark of a wandering dog, and then the silence returned.

Dessie reached over gently and, almost shyly, caressed his shoulder. She touched his forehead and his lips and kissed his eyelids. He turned toward her, and they kissed. He reached out slowly and tenderly to fondle her breasts.

He remembered her breasts when she was a girl, small and satiny smooth, with nipples like the buds of tiny flowers. Now her breasts had lost the firmness of youth, but he still loved touching them because he loved her.

"Aren't you too tired to play?" he asked. "You've been on your feet all day, and you must be exhausted."

"I'm fine," she said. "I even feel a little horny." She paused. "You know it's been almost a month."

"That long?" he feigned surprise.

They moved closer, their bodies not as quick and agile, no longer as impetuous or passionate. But through a lifetime together, they had grown familiar with one another, knew every movement, every response.

His body grew taut against her flesh, strained for what seemed only seconds, and then sagged away. His pulse beat more slowly.

"It gets weaker and quicker all the time," he sighed.

"Don't worry about it, honey," Dessie said. "We've had so much rousing, riotous lovemaking. In many ways, I prefer this now."

"You're just trying to make me feel better on my birthday."

"I'm not fooling," she said. "I can't stand the lightning and thunder anymore. If we go at it too hard, my back hurts and I get cramps in my legs and an ache in my abdomen."

They both laughed. Then they lay together in silence.

"Goodnight, my darling," Dessie said sleepily. "I hope we share many more healthy birthdays with the kids." In another moment she was asleep, her breathing soft and slow.

Andreas closed his eyes but could not sleep. He slipped quietly from the bed, trying not to disturb Dessie, and went to sit by the open windows. He inhaled the fragrance of the early summer night, the scents of flowers and leafy trees. The luminous moon faded and then reappeared from the haven of clouds. He stared down at the outline of the lighter houses alongside the ones that were charcoal black. A few lights were visible in the second-floor windows. He imagined people turning down their sheets, slipping into bed, perhaps to love as he and Dessie had loved, or to remain wakeful in their thoughts, and finally to sleep.

In the haunting moment that climaxed his day, he recalled his nostalgia in the library for his youthful love of books, the passion of

Karoll at his work, the mounds of his parents' and his son's graves, the buoyancy of his grandchildren, the glittering candles on the cake, fewer by far than the years he had lived, the consolation of Dessie's body . . . all of these suddenly coalesced to provide him a startling clarity of vision.

He saw himself as an aging man in a shadowed bedroom, his wife asleep with her head dark against the white swell of the pillow. They lived within a house, in a neighborhood of the city, within a country that was part of the planet Earth. He felt the two of them linked to the miracle of having been born and to the wisdom of death. They would someday be interred in the layers of earth, as the strata of epochs that had passed contained the shells of lizards and the bones of kings. In that way, Dessie would someday be drawn closer to the soul of her dead child, and he would dwell near the spirits of his parents with eternity to earn their forgiveness, and all of them would become part of the hallowed earth that held the dust of Socrates and Homer.

Trembling with the wonder and symmetry of the vision, he returned to bed. He moved gently closer to Dessie until their bodies were nested together.

A moment before he fell asleep, he recalled the lines from the poem of Yeats that Karoll had recited. Slowly, with a fervor born of that revelatory moment in time, he whispered the words into the night.

"And therefore I have sailed the seas and come / To the holy city of Byzantium."

This is another story that blends the factual and the fictional. My mother, the wife of my priest-father, was a compassionate woman and also an enterprising one. She caused my father and the church board of trustees a good deal of anguish because, if she saw someone in need, she would not wait for the conventional community methods of assistance. She never ruled anyone out as unworthy of help.

When I was a boy, in a time when prejudice was still rampant, I recall there was a young Greek girl married to a black soldier and remember the vigorous battle my mother fought with the community on their behalf. I cannot honestly say how their story worked out, but I fear the worst. Their union took place before Rosa Parks refused a seat in the rear of the bus and when a black man could be lynched for looking too brazenly at a white woman.

The older I become, the more I remember with awe the dimensions of my mother's remarkably expansive heart that encompassed all of mankind's suffering. I have often thought that if Judas had appeared at our door, she would have invited him in and sympathetically listened to his side of the story.

A Tale of Color

IN THESE DAYS WHEN REASONABLE MEN AND WOMEN accept the fairness of civil rights and arguments revolve more around the quotas of affirmative action, the story of Denzel and Sofia may seem old-fashioned. I think it is still timely today because marriage between the races continues to evoke hostility and even hatred. Yet my mother's efforts to help these two young people so many years ago were not made in the name of civil rights but because she thought it was the moral and compassionate thing to do.

I first heard the story told by my mother when I was a child. She narrated it to my older sisters, but it made a more lasting impression on me. In the years that followed, she retold it many times. When I knew the story by heart, my mother continued filling in the details that gave the story more substance.

The events began in the early 1950s, following World War II. A black U.S. Army soldier named Denzel Barnes, stationed in Greece with U.S. forces, met a young Greek village girl named Sofia. Black

26

soldiers had fought with Greek partisans and were regarded as friends and allies. Sofia's parents did not object when she accompanied Denzel to dances at the army post. The soldier and the Greek girl fell in love, and in the spring of 1952 they were married.

After receiving his discharge, Denzel and Sofia lived in the village while he worked on the farm of Sofia's brother. A year after they had married, his wife gave birth to a baby boy they named Nikolaos after Sofia's father.

Greece was still recovering from the terrible civil war that had followed World War II and had devastated the country. Life in the villages was harsh and barren. Although Denzel was strong and able to work hard from dawn to dusk, his labor barely met his family's basic needs.

Denzel was also homesick. In the evenings by the light of the oil lamp, he told Sofia about America. He described the lakefront in the city of Chicago, which had been his home. He told her of the ball games played on summer afternoons and of the barbecues on summer evenings. He told her of the jazz clubs where wild, spirit-lifting music was played all night. The more Denzel described America, the more nostalgic he became for the life he had known. Because Sofia loved him, she agreed to go home with him to America.

For a year, Denzel worked weekends and evenings to save the money for their fare. In the early spring of 1954, they said farewell to Sofia's family and traveled by bus to Athens. From the port of Piraeus they booked passage on a Greek ship bound for New York. From there they traveled by train to Chicago, where Denzel's parents lived. It was shortly after they arrived in Chicago that my mother met them for the first time.

"I really met Sofia first," my mother said. "She came to your father's parish church with her baby one Sunday morning, not long after she arrived in the city. Cleon Dussias—you remember, he owned the Athens Grocery—introduced her to me. She was a sweet and pretty girl who was already very homesick. Cleon thought I might help her get settled and perhaps help her meet some other young people in our parish.

"At the end of the service, I took Sofia and her son up to the sanctuary. Your father blessed the baby and gave him communion.

The following weekend, I had Sofia and her husband come to our apartment for dinner. It was then we learned that she had married a black man."

My mother had a balanced and tolerant nature that fully accepted the diversity of life. But she understood that her tolerance was not shared by many others. The intermarriage of races evoked hostility and outrage within as well as outside their parish community.

"Such prejudice was absurd," my mother said. "The only important thing was that a man and woman love and care for one another. It was hard for me to understand how people could resent them. They were such a striking couple. Sofia had long, dark hair and great dark eyes. Her husband was tall with a strong, muscular body. The baby, who seemed to combine his mother's beauty and his father's strength, was a treasure.

"I could also see right away that they were very much in love. When Sofia laughed or spoke, or when she held the baby in her arms, her husband watched her with adoration."

Knowing the couple faced serious problems, my mother appointed herself their patron and vowed to help them in any way she could. She had a reputation as a rebel herself (despite being the wife of the parish priest), and I think she might even have taken a certain pride in defying community norms.

"They had found housing by the week in a shabby one-room kitchenette apartment," my mother said, "but they could not afford anything better until Denzel found work. I spoke to several of our parishioners who owned buildings about renting the family an apartment. They were afraid to move an interracial couple into buildings occupied only by whites. But we did find Denzel a job as a third helper on the Open Hearth through Despina's cousin, Sam, who was a foreman in the South Chicago Steel Works. Denzel and Sofia were able to rent a small frame house in the vicinity of the mills."

Those neighborhoods around the mills were ethnic enclaves with little forbearance for other ethnic groups, let alone another race. But the mating of two races seemed to incite a more virulent fury. On two occasions, Sofia and Denzel had their windows broken by stones. But they held on until one night someone set a fire under their front porch. That angered Denzel, but at the same time he feared for his family's safety. While they looked for other lodgings, he and Sofia and the baby moved in with his parents on the South Side.

"But they had problems there as well," my mother said. "The neighborhood was totally black, and many of his parents' neighbors had as much trouble accepting a white girl in their midst as the white people in other neighborhoods had in accepting Denzel. In truth, those two young people were outcasts, suspended between two worlds, neither of which would accept them.

"Now you have to remember that in those years, the races were strictly divided. This was long before the Reverend Martin Luther King touched the consciences of people and the civil rights struggles brought some beneficent change in America."

Sofia and Denzel came to rely on my mother's friendship. She invited them to church and community affairs. She watched over them diligently, her vigilant and righteous eye stifling any hostile murmurs or glares of resentment. "Remember what it was like when the first Greek immigrants came to this country!" she sternly reminded parish members. "We fought prejudice against our people then! Now we should not forget those struggles. If we cannot accept these young people for who they are, we have no right to call ourselves Christians!"

Not long after Sofia and Denzel moved into his parents' house, Denzel's mother invited my mother and father to dinner. My mother remembered that first dinner as tense and uncomfortable.

"Denzel's father and mother were truly good people," my mother said. "Mr. Barnes worked as a mailman and Mrs. Barnes as a hospital aide. Their house was very small, and they were self-conscious about the things they didn't have. They tried to make us feel welcome, but they were not accustomed to having white people in their house."

My mother understood that it was even hard for them to feel at ease around Sofia. A lifetime of fearing and resenting whites left them not knowing how to accept her.

"They tried, I know they tried," my mother said, "but our society with its prejudices and its intolerances had done its work too well."

To reinforce the bonds between the families, my mother also invited Denzel and Sofia and his parents to Sunday dinner in our house. That dinner also proved strained and difficult.

My mother invited them again, a few weeks later. Denzel was a little late in coming from his shift at the mills and Sofia was tending the baby in another room when Denzel's father told my parents that his son and Sofia would have to find another place to live.

"Imagine the anguish of a father having to say that his son and his wife and grandchild would have to leave his house," my mother said. "I will never forget the grief in that man's face and voice. But he and his wife lived in a black neighborhood where they were shielded against the prejudice and fear they faced each day in white neighborhoods. At night they returned to their own house, which had always been their sanctuary. But it was no longer a sanctuary. Seeing the way their neighbors responded to Sofia and their grandchild was a constant reminder to Mr. Barnes of the bigotry of his own people.

"But even worse than the bigotry was his fear of some violence," my mother said. "Mr. Barnes was afraid that some black man who had suffered injury at the hands of whites might harm Sofia or the baby. He was also afraid that Denzel might become enraged at some offense to his family and commit some violence that would put him in jail."

My mother had witnessed and experienced a great deal of sadness in her life. Yet she could not recount the details of that night without an old heartache assailing her face and voice.

"That night when Denzel arrived at our apartment," my mother said, "his father told him and Sofia what he had earlier told us. Denzel was sorely hurt by what he felt to be his father's rejection. I will not forget the wound visible in his eyes. Nor will I forget the way he spoke to all of us, his words full of bitterness and yet with a dignity as well. He told his father and mother in front of us that somewhere a beginning had to be made, a beginning that would give black and white a chance to live together in peace.

"His father told Denzel he accepted that what his son was saying was just and true. But it was not yet time, not in his neighborhood and not in his house. They would have to find a place among others who were trying to make such a beginning."

Denzel's mother wept then. My mother tried to console her and wept with her. Skilled in the reassurances of his faith, my father sought the words to comfort them.

"I have listened to your father's sermons many times," my mother said. "His faith was strong and his words, born of that faith, were often true. But that night the words he spoke were hollow. I think he understood for that problem at that time, God's solution was not one men would accept."

My mother returned zealously to the task of finding Denzel and Sofia another place to live. She had helped so many people in our community, visiting them while sick, attending their problems and concerns. Now she exerted every effort and called up all those outstanding debts. She finally found them a small, shabby coach house on the far west side of the city owned by a Greek man obligated to my mother. He agreed to rent it to Denzel and Sofia. The dwelling was in a polyglot neighborhood where poverty outweighed prejudice. For the first time since arriving in the city, Denzel and Sofia were able to live in peace.

But the coach house was old and the windows drafty. The only heat in the single large room came from a wood-burning stove. During the winter's cold days and frigid nights, Sofia and the baby huddled beside the stove or remained in bed swathed under blankets.

That winter the baby, Nikolaos, became ill. My mother moved quickly to get the child to a doctor. The infant was diagnosed as having severe bronchitis, and the doctor recommended they move from the damp, cold coach house. He also suggested they locate in a drier, warmer climate.

"They could barely afford to live where they were," my mother said. "They had no money for any kind of move. I would have helped if I could, but our own family, your sisters and you, required all our resources."

In an effort to find them a more accommodating place to live, my mother once again returned to the pursuit. But hard as she tried, she could not find anything suitable. In the early spring, a temporary solution was found that required the family to split up. Sofia and her baby moved in with a kind Greek family who provided her a room and private bath in a comfortable suburban house with a yard and a garden. Denzel moved into the dormitory of a YMCA and visited Sofia and his son on the weekends.

"That spring while they lived separated from one another, I would take the train to the suburbs to visit Sofia and the baby," my mother said. "The house where they lived was very nice and the people were good to them, but the baby was still ailing. Sofia herself had grown thinner and weaker. She was lonely for Denzel and unhappy and, for the first time, talked longingly to me of Greece. She felt the sun and the clean country air of the village would heal the baby and help her regain her strength as well."

Yet as hard and unsatisfying as life in Chicago was for them, Denzel saw no future for himself in the village. But he recognized the benefits the change would have for his family. They decided Sofia would take the baby back to Greece. Denzel had saved a little money from his wages, and my mother helped with a loan from a friend. Meanwhile, Denzel would continue working in Chicago until he had saved enough money to buy a small house. Then he would arrange to bring his family back to America.

"Neither of them wanted to break up the family," my mother said. "But they had little choice. The baby and Sofia were ill. They could not live together anyway, and this course of action offered them a shred of hope.

"The day before Sofia and Nikolaos were to leave for New York to board a ship for Greece," my mother said, "your father held a service for them in the church. Denzel's parents came and half a dozen people from our parish who had grown fond of the family. There were also a few of Denzel's friends from the steel mills. Your father gave them his blessing and wished them well and told them God would help them someday reunite with happiness."

My mother went with them to the train station on the day Sofia and the baby departed.

"It is a scene I have remembered so many times," my mother said. "Denzel held his wife and their baby in his arms as if none of the multitude of people in the station existed. Both of them were crying, and the baby, not really understanding, of course, was crying too. Sofia spoke of the baby growing healthy and strong again. Denzel kept repeating his vow that he would work hard and send for them as soon as he could.

"When the train started to pull out of the station," my mother continued, "Denzel walked alongside the window where Sofia sat holding his son, his hand reaching up as though he were trying to pierce the glass. Sofia had her hand pressed against the window, as well. The train kept moving and Denzel kept walking alongside, having to walk more quickly as the train picked up speed. Finally, he broke into a run, his hand still outstretched toward his family, until I lost sight of him in the crowd on the platform.

"Long after the train was gone," my mother said, "I waited on the platform for Denzel to return. Kostas Sarantis, who had brought us to the station, was waiting to drive us to the South Side. But Denzel never returned. After a while I thought that perhaps in his grief he had wanted to be alone, and we left."

Although Sofia promised to write, my mother didn't hear from her. She also lost touch with Denzel, although she tried several times to contact him. He had left his job at the mills and had also broken off contact with his parents. My mother did not know the names of Sofia's parents and was not even sure about the village where they lived except that it was somewhere in the Peloponnesus of Greece.

Years passed and my mother never heard from either Sofia or Denzel again. Because she was a strong believer in the old virtues and in the rewards of faith and fidelity, she felt that, somehow, overcoming those forces that sought to divide them, the family of three had been reunited. Near the end of her life, she envisioned them living somewhere in Greece, surrounded by children and grandchildren, sustaining a happy, fulfilled old age.

"I understand all the difficulties they faced," my mother said. "But you had to be with me in the station. You had to see the devotion in their faces to understand how deep and abiding was their love. Such love could conquer any obstacle."

Perhaps my mother was right. After all, I had not been present in the station with Denzel and Sofia and their baby and had not witnessed their final moments together. I also recognized the power of love and knew that a bond as strong as theirs might well have prevailed.

But life does not always provide a felicitous conclusion. I have to believe that if Denzel and Sofia had been reunited, my mother would have heard from them. In the absence of any word from either of them, what seemed most likely was that, driven by futility and despair, Denzel never returned to Greece to bring his family back to America, and he and Sofia and their baby were never reunited.

My mother was their witness and deeply felt their pain and sorrow. In the many times she related their story to me, she communicated the intensity of her emotion.

But I have lived long enough to understand that the suffering and separation of a black man and a young Greek girl and their child might not even earn a footnote in the long, sorrowful chronicle of racial intolerance and hate.

One of the Greek tragedians, perhaps Euripides, has written that "in the theater of human life, it is only for gods and angels to remain spectators."

Solon is, unfortunately, a participant who does not realize that life cannot be neatly categorized, that reason can be a leaky ship, and that in the mysterious relationship between men and women, every action sets in motion a series of stunning, often bewildering consequences. Solon has chosen his bed, and it would take a better writer than I am to get him out of it.

The Wisdom of Solon

WHEN SOLON PANOS FIRST SAW THE YOUNG WOMAN in church on the Holy Friday before Easter, he understood why he had waited fifty years to get married. She stood across the center aisle from his pew, a simple black dress sheathing her slender body. Her lovely face illuminated in the halo of the white candle she held before her, the tiny flame glistening across her long, raven-dark hair. He was also moved by the sweetness of her voice as she sang the hymns.

At the end of the Holy Service, as the parishioners passed Father Basil to receive a small white carnation he gave each one, Solon lingered in his pew so he could watch the young woman descending the aisle. She walked gracefully through the aura of candles and incense. Solon was bewildered at the tremor that raced through his body and wondered, suddenly, whether the weeks of fasting might have made him lightheaded.

He followed her down the aisle from the church into the night, desperately seeking another glimpse of her. Outside the church she blended into the crowd surging toward the parking lot.

When he had unhappily accepted that he had lost her, he saw her at one of the porticos with Elias and Aspasia Vodantis, two members of the parish whom Solon knew well. In the past he had served on the parish council with Elias.

In a resolute effort to get closer to them, Solon pushed through the crowd more aggressively than his normal courtesy would have permitted. In his haste, he elbowed aside a prim-looking matron who obstructed his path. She glared at him, and he murmured a heartfelt apology.

Just a few feet from the trio, he was seized with panic because he did not wish to appear to be thrusting himself into their midst. He was saved by seeing an acquaintance nearby. Solon greeted the man loudly enough for his voice to carry. Elias heard him and waved him closer.

"Good to see you, Solon," Elias said warmly. He was a short, bald man with bright eyes and the body of an Attica bull. At one time he had owned three successful restaurants, but business reverses had caused him to close two of them. His wife, Aspasia, was a lean-fleshed, tense woman who always appeared to be anticipating unhappy tidings.

Solon shook hands with Elias and cordially greeted Aspasia. Only then did he permit himself to look directly at the young woman. He found her even more beautiful than she had appeared in church. Her skin was flawless, her lips shapely, her teeth even and extraordinarily white. A strand of dark hair had fallen across her cheek, and Solon resisted a reckless impulse to reach out and gently push the vagrant curl aside.

"This is our daughter, Angelina," Elias said. "She is an actress who has been living in Los Angeles. She has come home to visit us for a little while."

"We haven't seen her in almost a year," Aspasia said, sighing. "We want her to stay, but she is eager to get back to California, you know, where they have the earthquakes."

"They have other things in California besides earthquakes, Mama," Angelina said quietly. Her voice was well-modulated, her words enunciated clearly. She extended her hand, and Solon took her fingers into his own much larger hand. The contact was light and fleeting, and yet he felt it as erotic as a caress.

They exchanged a few more pleasantries, and then the family moved toward their car. Solon would have gladly walked with them, but his car was parked in the opposite direction. All he could do was stand under the pale crescent of the Easter moon and watch them move away. Solon softly repeated the name "Angelina" several times, the syllables emerging from his lips like a song.

Back in his apartment that night, despite his weariness and the lateness of the hour, Solon could not sleep. He rose several times from his bed and tried to read, but the words eluded him. When he returned to bed and closed his eyes, he was besieged by a memory of Angelina in church. The sacred firmament had been a proscenium for her wounding beauty. He saw her dark eyes again, hinting at the mysteries women's eyes had concealed since the age of Eve.

He was suddenly, starkly conscious of the absence of love in his life. A year had passed since his relationship had ended with Patricia Moriarty, a lovely Irish accountant who had worked for Solon in his wholesale coffee company. He had been fond of her and they had enjoyed attending dinners and theaters together, but he had never seriously considered marriage. After a while, they had parted by mutual consent. Shortly afterward, she also had left his employ.

Before Patricia, there had been another intimate friendship with Tereza, an attractive widow with two teenaged children. She lived across the city and attended a different Greek church. Their relationship had lasted about two years. Toward the end, Solon had sensed Tereza was depressed because he had not broached the subject of marriage. But Solon had been careful not to make her any promises or to encourage her into believing he might be contemplating such a momentous commitment. At that point he had felt it wiser to end their relationship. A few months later, he had seen Tereza at a diocese social event and was pleased that she did not seem to harbor any ill feelings.

Those relationships, as well as his previous romances, had involved sex as well as companionship. When intimacy was required, Solon made love with sufficient vigor that it earned him the praise of the women for his virility. He enjoyed the moments of passion and release. At the same time, the months of abstinence between relationships did not trouble him. He was grateful that he was not harassed by sexual obsessions as many men were. In the Greek pantheon of moderation, sex was an ornament and not a pillar of life.

But now in the passage of his sleepless night, he was forced to admit that his romances had been monotonously similar and ultimately unsatisfying. He would be caught up in a momentary attraction, and after a while, it would be over. None of the affairs had been marked by passionate love. He understood that was because his relationships had been conducted as he lived, with continence and restraint.

Reason and moderation had been the guiding forces of his life. His parents (may their souls forever rest in peace) had named him for Solon, the great fifth century B.C. Athenian lawgiver and social reformer who had given all male citizens, including the poorest, the right to vote in the assembly and in the jury-courts.

Solon had always prided himself that in his life and work, he continued that tradition of reason manifested by the ancient Greeks from the time of Socrates. Reason was the divine ruler of the universe and separated men from the animals. In the philosophy of the Stoics and in the Gospel of St. John, it became incarnate as the Word of God. A man disregarded the counsel of reason at his peril.

But now, on this Holy Friday that marked the entombment of Jesus Christ, he recognized that his life had been entombed, as well. Awakened by the vision of Angelina, he saw clearly that without the inspiration of true, endearing love, he had fallen from one shallow relationship to another.

Yet, as with the resurrection of the Savior, for the first time in his fifty years he felt wondrously reborn. He understood that he must be experiencing the enchantment of love. Although he had no precedent for that exalted emotion, he had read enough of the grand passions of men and women to understand that was what had happened to him.

He remained exhilarated as the first frail light of dawn appeared around the shades. Through a partially open window, he heard the clear, sweet song of a thrush. As he drifted wearily into sleep, he recalled having read that when one loved for the first time, the world of the first rose and the first bird's song was reborn.

When Solon woke later that morning, although he had slept only several hours, he felt refreshed. He rose buoyantly from his bed. While the coffee brewed, he shaved and showered. Afterward, eating a light breakfast, he carefully considered the merits and liabilities he would bring to any courtship of Angelina.

There was, of course, the initial difference in their ages. Solon was fifty years old. While he could not be sure, he doubted that

Angelina was any more than twenty-nine or thirty. Yet two decades between them was not an irreconcilable difference. He knew of half a dozen men in the parish who had married much younger wives and who seemed to have happy marriages.

Belying his age, he was in the physical condition of a much younger man. He exercised diligently and was careful about what he ate and drank. His weight had not varied in a decade, and his blood pressure and cholesterol levels were excellent.

In addition to being in exemplary health, he was successful and affluent. His coffee-importing business was growing, and a sales force of thirty representatives sold his product throughout the Midwest. He was well respected in the community and admired as a major contributor to many worthy causes. He was also regarded as a very eligible bachelor. On a number of occasions in the past, he had been approached by matchmakers on behalf of a family who desired him for one of their daughters.

When he first asked Elias Vodantis if he might invite Angelina out for dinner, the man was surprised and obviously pleased. His wife, Aspasia, wasn't initially responsive to Solon (he believed it was the matter of his age), but she had to admit he was a serious and well-qualified suitor.

Solon even drove to Joliet to meet Angelina's brother, Paulo, who seemed quite happy at the prospect of having a wealthy businessman as his brother-in-law. Paulo, who was married with a young child, appeared to be having a hard time in operating his lunchroom and making a profit. Solon vowed he'd find a way to help him.

When Solon first asked Angelina to go to dinner with him, she had been alerted by her parents and didn't appear surprised. He had the initial feeling that she was less interested in him as a suitor than flattered by his attentions because it gave her a certain importance in the eyes of her parents. Solon understood he would have a brief window of opportunity to impress her before she lost interest.

Throughout that spring and the early part of summer, Solon conducted his courtship of Angelina in the way a general might manage a major campaign. He was a strong believer in *arete*, which meant virtue. Virtue combined with courage, as defined by the great Aristotle, was the middle point of prudence between the extremes of cowardice and rashness.

In all his dealings with the family, Solon sought to maintain that middle ground of prudence. He was courteous and considerate to all of them. He brought flowers for Angelina and wine and cheese for her parents each time he visited their house. When Elias confided in him that his son, Paulo, would be closing his restaurant and looking for other work, Solon offered the young man a position as one of his sales representatives with a proven and lucrative territory. Hearing that Elias was seeking a sizable loan from the Central Bank where Solon had several accounts, he spoke to the bank president about guaranteeing the loan with his own signature. Elias was grateful to the point of tears.

The first sign Solon had that Angelina might be responding favorably to his courtship was when she delayed her return to California, first by a week and then by another month. They continued going to elegant restaurants for dinner and then to concerts and plays.

They began to share confidences. Angelina told him of an unhappy love affair she'd had with a man near her own age.

"Young men are like bulls," she said. "They are intent only on pleasing themselves. They find it hard to love because they are so in love with themselves."

She also spoke to Solon of her struggles as an actress.

"You gather with twenty other aspiring actresses for an audition," she told Solon bitterly. "It is like a meat market. You wait your turn until they give you a moment to read a few lines. Then they send you away with a promise they will call. But they never call. I always felt they knew who they were going to choose, some friend of the director or of the producer, from the beginning." She paused. "I think, sometimes, that I am ready now to move on to other things."

Solon listened to her confidences with sympathy. He confided in her that he too had reached a point in his life where he sought new challenges. He had proven his success in business and was ready to move on. In addition to his investments, the sale of his business would net him several million dollars. For a year or two, before settling on some new enterprise, he considered traveling around the world. He asked her if she had ever cruised the Greek islands. She told him she had not.

"It is a magic adventure unlike any other delight, Angelina," Solon told her. "There are more than two thousand islands and inlets that the Greeks call 'flowers of marble.' Legend has it they were formed from the scattered limbs of a god who fell from the sky." He paused and carefully reached across the table to gently touch her hand. "Perhaps someday I can show those islands to you."

He savored the way she listened, a range of expressions lighting her cheeks and eyes.

The sharing of confidences drew them closer, and he felt her warming to him. After they had been going out together for almost two months, one evening, while taking her home, he was emboldened to kiss her, tasting the sweetness of walnuts and wine on her lips. A feeling of exhilaration raced through his body when he felt her responding.

At the end of the summer, Solon sought the approval of Elias and Aspasia so he might ask Angelina to marry him. Both her parents had grown fond of him and expressed their delight at the prospect of the union. The following evening, over an elegant dinner with Angelina in a fine downtown restaurant, Solon formally proposed. Angelina stared at him for a long moment and then reached across the table to clasp his hand.

"I will now tell you the truth, Solon," she said softly. "In the beginning I was certain that nothing would ever take place between us. But being with you these last months, seeing the respect and affection with which you have treated my family and me, I know you are a good and sincere man. I have come to care for you. Perhaps it is time for me to put aside childish dreams. So, dear Solon. I will be happy to become your wife."

At that moment, his courtship successful, he was so full of love that he could not restrain his tears. When she saw the tears in his eyes, Angelina wept as well. He felt their hearts bonded and their souls linked as one.

They were married on the fifteenth of September in a large wedding followed by a lavish reception in the Grand Ballroom of the downtown Hilton. Five hundred friends and well-wishers attended, all of them witness to the splendor and elegance of the affair. Elias, as the father of the bride, was expected to pay for the wedding. But knowing his future father-in-law's financial straits, Solon, discreetly careful about any possible affront to the man's pride, had beseeched Elias to allow him to pay for the wedding. He swore no one would ever know. His father-in-law embraced Solon and called him a "truly generous and caring man."

On their wedding night in the bridal suite of the hotel, Angelina told Solon she hoped he wasn't unhappy because she'd had a few other lovers.

"I have had a few other loves too," he told her.

"But men feel differently, don't they?" Angelina asked. "Men want their women to enter marriage as virgins."

"I cannot speak for other men," Solon reassured her, "but it would not be reasonable to expect that at your age, young and healthy as you are, you would not have loved others."

"Oh, Solon," she whispered. "You are a truly good man. And I promise I will try to make you a loving and devoted wife."

When they undressed and got into bed, Solon was a gentle and considerate lover with his bride. In response to his caresses, she seemed restrained and almost shy. But after they were both aroused, he was a little surprised at the wellsprings of passion she revealed.

The following day, with her parents, his best man, Peter Poulos, and a few close friends, they had a festive farewell lunch. Afterward, a limousine picked them up for O'Hare, where they flew first class to begin their honeymoon in Greece. At Piraeus that same evening, they boarded a luxurious cruise ship for a fourteen-day cruise of the Greek islands.

Their first evening at sea, they dined at the captain's table, and Solon charmed everyone by his eloquence in praise of his wife's beauty.

When they returned to their stateroom, Solon was weary and pleased at how well the evening had gone. He was also full of wine and rich food and would have been grateful to sleep. He was a little dismayed when Angelina seemed eager to make love. He felt compelled to oblige her and was briefly caught up in their shared passion. Afterward, for the first time he could ever recall in any of his previous relationships, he was forced to continue caressing Angelina long after his own desire was satisfied.

The days that followed began early in the morning with their descending into the dinghies that carried them from the ship to the shore. The blue-black water was clear as glass, and the floor of the sea could be seen through fathomless depths.

The islands were as beautiful as Solon remembered, and he had the added delight of sharing their beauty with Angelina. They landed in enchanting harbors with fishing caïques and colorful sailboats moored in sight of the shops and seaside *tavernas*. On the lower slopes of the mountain above the harbor were clustered the brilliantly white houses with red-tiled roofs. Higher on the mountain were the white-washed churches with their crosses and the tiny chapels dedicated to St. Nicholas, patron saint of sailors.

In his earlier visits to the islands, Solon had set his own pace. He'd spend an hour or so touring in the morning and then the balance of the afternoon sitting leisurely in one of the seaside cafés, sipping an ouzo and enjoying the activity around him.

But Angelina was an inquisitive tourist, eager to go everyplace and to see everything. They spent the full day touring monuments and ruins, visiting bazaars and street markets. A brief respite for lunch in a pleasant seaside café was all too soon interrupted by the relentless cacophony of the tour guide urging them on their way.

By the afternoon of the fourth day, on their fourth island, Solon had had enough. It seemed to him he had already spent weeks trudging up cobbled streets, past terra cotta terraces, fighting off the entreaties of souvenir vendors. He had never realized before how many ruined temples, drums of columns, and fragments of broken colonnades existed everywhere in Greece. He also began to perceive the landscape in a way he had never seen it before. He noted the absence of trees and how often only a thin, gray-green fuzz of shrubbery softened the cracked and wrinkled rocks, giving the landscape a naked and austere look.

Every fleeting moment they paused to rest was quickly assaulted by the buoyant cries of the guide urging them on to another site. Solon had to resist giving the relentlessly energetic bellwether a blow on the side of his noisy head.

But only he seemed to harbor a silent complaint. Everyone else appeared as enthusiastic and willing as Angelina to race around and see as much as possible.

By the conclusion of the endless day, Solon yearned only to take a hot shower, to climb wearily into bed, and, above all else, God willing, to sleep. But stimulated and enchanted by the sights she had witnessed during the day, each night Angelina was passionately avid to make love. The islands seemed to provide her some indefatigable reserve of energy that made her grow stronger and more vigorous each day. She also grew bolder and more unrestrained in her lovemaking.

Once, after they had finished making love, Angelina rolled over against his body, clasping Solon tightly.

"I love you, Solon!" she whispered fervently. "Every day is full of new beauty! I am so happy, my darling, and I love you so much!"

He was moved at her devotion and tenderly kissed her cheek.

"Tell me you love me!"

"Of course I love you, my dearest," Solon said.

"How much?"

"Very much!" he said emphatically.

"Tell me!" she insisted. "Tell me something more!"

"I love you very much, my dearest," he repeated.

"Tell me more! Tell me what you want to do to me!"

He cleared his throat uneasily.

"I want to love you," he said. "I want to make love to you."

"Is that all?" she asked urgently. "What else? What other indecent things do you want to do to me?"

"I want to caress you," he said, trying not to disappoint her. "I want to caress you and make love to you . . ."

"What else!" she persisted. "What else do you want to do to me? Tell me!"

He understood there were things she wanted him to say, but he had never spoken such words to any woman before. His throat would not release them. She pressed closer to him. He felt her breast and thigh, hard as marble, forged against his body.

"I will whisper in your ear what I wish you would do to me," she said. "Come closer . . ."

A little nervously he shifted closer. He felt her hot breath on his ear. He resolved not to be surprised at anything she said.

Yet, he was shocked. He had never heard words and phrases like that from a woman before.

"Angelina," he said, and he could not keep a tone of reproach from his voice. Her only response was a deep, husky laugh that seemed to come from another woman's throat.

The endless days of sightseeing, climbing mountains, and inspecting ruins continued. For the first time in his life, Solon admitted to himself that he had wearied of classical Greece. On Santorini, the volcanic island, they scaled the mountain on the backs of donkeys, ascending the 700-foot precipitous slope to the town of Thira on the peak. He felt a pronounced sympathy for the wretched beasts that spent their days carting corpulent tourists up the steep mountain.

On Mykonos, Angelina marveled at the multitude of white-painted windmills that dotted the landscape, while he lamented the hordes of unwashed, boisterous youths that filled the tavernas. On the island of Delos they followed the guide to the terrace of legendary lions carved in archaic style of white Naxian marble, their lithe, lean bodies stretched toward the sky. Close by was the dried-up sacred lake and the drums of columns that had once formed the Temple of Apollo.

The day was hot and Solon felt weak and faint but concealed it from Angelina and the other passengers. That evening, back on the ship, he ate only a light salad and then excused himself, saying he had postcards he wished to write. He hoped that by the time Angelina and the others had finished dinner, he would be sound asleep.

In his suite he hastily wrote a few cards, then undressed and climbed gratefully into bed. He fell asleep the moment his burdened head felt the pillow.

He did not know how long he slept, nor did he hear Angelina enter their cabin. He wakened reluctantly to her soft voice whispering in his ear.

"Solon . . . are you asleep?"

He kept his eyes tightly closed and did not move.

She tugged gently at his arm.

"My darling," she said. "Oh my darling." She tugged harder at him. Fearing she might think he had suffered a heart attack and call for help, he opened his eyes.

"Angelina," he said through his drowsiness, "my dearest, I guess I was just more exhausted than I realized . . ."

She did not answer but bent still closer, her hand groping under the covers toward his loins.

"My darling," she whispered. "I want you so much."

With a mute groan he realized there was no escape. He twisted himself out of the covers and reached for his wife. She leaped eagerly into his arms.

Later, with his limbs aching, his body stiff and sore, he listened with bewilderment to the sound of Angelina singing in the shower. He had the eerie and distressing feeling that she was draining him of strength to reinforce her own energy.

On the tenth day of their cruise, rough seas prevented their boarding the dinghies for a shore excursion. Solon gratefully looked forward to a day without having to scale a ruin or climb a mountain. After breakfast, when Angelina went to one of the pools to swim with some acquaintances they had met onboard, Solon fled to a deck chair in a remote part of the ship and sat down with his well-worn copy of Homer's *Odyssey*. He made a halfhearted effort to read, but his eyes kept closing. He dozed and was startled awake by a steward bending over his chair.

"Mr. Panos," the steward said courteously, "your wife is requesting that you come to your cabin."

He thanked the man and rose to walk slowly and wearily toward his cabin. He found Angelina, invigorated by her swim, waiting for him. In another moment they were making love.

Hoping to gain a momentary respite from his nightly filial obligations and thinking enough wine might render Angelina lethargic and sleepy, the following night he kept refilling his wife's wine glass from the decanter. She never showed the slightest trace of intoxication. As for her desire, that seemed escalated and amplified. Her passion exhausted him, and by the end of their lovemaking that night, he feared he might pass out.

On the fourteenth and final day of the cruise, they spent a particularly exhausting span of hours climbing a precipitous peak. By the time the day was finished, Solon was wearier than he had been in his life. He came out of the hot shower, resolved to tell Angelina that he was not feeling well and needed to rest. Besides, they would be docking in Piraeus in the morning and would need to rise early. Prudence suggested they get some sleep.

But when he saw her disappointed face, ardent with love and amorous with anticipation, he was ashamed of his deception and took her into his arms.

But the long, exhausting days and the sexually active nights had finally taken their toll. For the first time since their wedding night, Solon could do nothing. His pride pushed him to several additional attempts, but he only replicated his initial failure.

Angelina was tolerant and understanding.

"I'm being selfish, I know, in wanting us to make love so often," she said with what seemed genuine remorse. "But don't be concerned. Sleep now, my darling, and tomorrow morning you'll be fine." Her voice trailed off into a suggestive whisper, a promise of delights postponed for just a few more hours.

In a few moments she was soundly, serenely asleep. But Solon could not sleep. Feeling the slight rocking of the ship beneath them, he lay with his body aching and exhausted, contemplating the weeks and months of desperate, ardent activity ahead of him. He bleakly accepted that the comfortable and orderly pattern that had marked his life had been shattered.

He considered for a moment that if Angelina became pregnant, he might gain a reprieve. But her passion was so strong that he suspected she would remain sexually active for as long as she could before her condition mandated abstinence. Then, after the birth of their child, the relentless cycle of action and exertion would start over again. He uttered a heartfelt and profound sigh.

Through the small curtained window, the Aegean moon cast shimmering beams across the cabin. It was the same moon that had shone down across the stately columns of the temples in which the sages of Greece had debated and discoursed on virtue, courage, honor, and pride.

All his life Solon had venerated those manifestations of reason. He had shunned imprudence and folly and had been, to the best of his ability, a temperate and rational man.

Yet in that revelatory moment, he realized that all his years of wisdom had been nullified by a single reckless and foolish act, his marriage to the younger, more vigorous, and much more sexually driven woman. That had been a foolhardy and indiscreet deed for which he would have to pay . . . and pay.

He sighed again and turned on his back. He folded his hands in resignation across his stomach, much in the way he would lie if he were in his coffin instead of in his bed.

When I was a boy, our family had a small, rustic cottage in the Chain-of-Lakes region of northern Illinois. My younger sister, Irene, and I spent many summers there under the care of a dear lady who had lived with our family for years and whom we called "Naka." My father would come out from Chicago for a day or two at a time to fish in nearby Fox Lake, but mostly we were alone, our days spent with a few other children, all of us lazy and carefree.

One summer a girl of about twenty came to visit a neighbor and, despite the difference in our ages, buoyantly played our childhood games with us for the period of a week. I cannot even remember her name, but she was a vision of beauty that I tried to capture in Christina. So this story is very close to being autobiographical. I have made a number of things up, of course, but to this day I remember the wind catching her dress and flipping it up to provide me a blinding glimpse of her naked legs and thighs. Even after all these years, that memory remains more erotic for me than much of the explicit sexual material one finds on the Internet today.

Christina's Summer

THE SUMMER I BECAME THIRTEEN, MY MOTHER, SISTER, and I stayed in our cottage in the Chain-of-Lakes region north of Chicago. We had been summering there from the time I was eight and my sister six. My father, who remembered the pastoral tranquillity of his village in Greece, felt that the country would be healthy for the family. He told us many times how fortunate we were; after all, he had to stay in the city to manage his grocery.

My father came to stay with us one weekend a month. On one of his visits, reclining in a lawn chair, a handkerchief tied around his forehead to absorb the sweat, he watched me playing.

"You've grown two inches taller this year," my father frowned. "You're too big a boy now to spend your days fooling around. Next summer you'll come to work with me in the store."

"And what will Despina and I do?" my mother asked.

"You can still come to the cottage," my father said.

"I'm not leaving Alex alone all summer in the city," my mother said quietly.

The exchange finished there, but I knew it meant we were spending our last summer at the lake.

The cottage we lived in from the start of summer until Labor Day was a square, unadorned frame structure that sat on wooden posts. It had originally been a large single room and was later divided by plasterboard partitions into tiny bedrooms, each one with barely enough space for a single bed and a small dresser. There was a narrow kitchen with a sink and a two-burner stove fueled by propane gas. There wasn't any electricity or running water in the cottage, and our only light came from kerosene lamps, which my mother used reluctantly because she feared fire. We went to bed at dusk and rose at dawn to wash, shivering in frigid water from a pump in the yard. For our natural functions, we used the small, drafty outhouse, domain of spiders and snakes, with a moon-shaped hole cut in a door whose rusted hinges creaked when it was opened.

We spent little time inside the cottage except to sleep. We either played outdoors or on the screen porch, which held a table, chairs, and swing. On Saturday nights, my mother sometimes allowed us to stay up after dark. She'd light one of the kerosene lamps, and in its flickering glow my sister and I played shadow games against the screens. Outside our porch, drawn to the light, moths flailed their wings against the mesh of the screens. Farther out in the darkness, crickets made their chirping sounds, and from time to time the night carried the plaintive cry of an owl.

We had no visitors all summer except for my father. I didn't mind the isolation, but I'm sure my mother was often lonely. Her only friend at the lake was our nearest neighbor, Mrs. Schroeder, who lived in a cottage down the road.

Our day began at dawn when we ate breakfast on our porch, bowls of hot oatmeal or corn flakes covered with blueberries we had picked from vines in the woods. Outside the cottage, early morning dewdrops glistened on the leaves and flowers. After breakfast our friends Greta and Jerry, Mrs. Schroeder's daughter and son, came over to play.

Greta was about my age, a robust girl with close-cropped brown hair. Her brother, near my sister's age, was skinny and had a sinus condition, so he was always sniveling. Despite the disparity in our years, we played amiably together in the woods and broad pasture where old man Murray grazed his cows. The solemn bovines ignored our racing and shouting, continuing to eat placidly while brushing away flies with their tails.

The four of us formed a disheveled, barefoot crew with a boundless terrain for our games. Beside the pasture, which was ideal for Run Chief Run, there was a patch of woods for Hide and Go Seek, and beyond the woods on a rise of hill lay the remains of a long-abandoned cemetery, its markers and tombstones crumbled in a tangle of leaf mold and worm-shaped roots that curled across the graves.

As a change from our games on land, we walked down to the channel and fished from the pier with old bamboo poles whose hooks we baited with worms. When we tired of that sedentary pastime, we climbed into the Schroeders' small drab rowboat moored at the pier and rowed in a circle around and around the narrow channel that led out to the lake where we were forbidden to go. At noon Mrs. Schroeder or my mother made us peanut butter and jelly sandwiches. Then we were on the loose again. When we were worn out from playing, we sprawled to rest at the base of the ghost tree in the pasture. We called it that because it bloomed only every other year, and that summer it loomed bare-branched and gaunt above our heads.

We lounged under the tree on a hot afternoon in early August when Greta jumped to her feet.

"Who wants to wrestle?" she asked, flexing her strong, sun-browned arms. She motioned a challenge to her brother.

"I don't wanna wrestle," Jerry protested. Against his wishes, Greta pulled him to his feet and, after a quick twist and shove, flopped him back to the ground where he laid sniveling and whimpering.

"How about you?" Greta asked my sister. "I'll wrestle you with one arm. I'll keep the other behind my back."

"I don't want to!" my sister said. When Greta made a threatening move toward her, Despina leaped to her feet and raced away. Greta shook her head in disgust and turned to me.

"How about it?" she asked.

Greta and I had been wrestling for years. She was stronger than I was and had humiliated me many times, strutting around afterward, smirking in triumph that rubbed salt in my wounds.

But each summer I had been getting stronger, and our last few contests had ended in draws with neither of us able to pin the other.

Goaded by her challenge yet half-afraid that she might whip me again, I rose to face her. We circled one another warily, our bodies tense and ready to pounce. From a safe distance my sister watched, and Jerry slid backward on the ground to get out of harm's way.

I grabbed for Greta, and she slapped my hand away. She made a move for me that I evaded. Another feint, and then our bodies rammed together in a wild flailing of arms. A panic seized me when I first felt her full strength, but I held my ground. We braced our legs and shoulders, straining against one another, and then she faltered. With a leaping surge of power I pushed harder, and her legs gave way. We sprawled on the ground, her body crushed beneath mine. She let out a short, tight cry of pain, and then I had her pinned to the ground, holding her arms above her head, looking triumphantly down at her face.

My sister clapped in approval and Jerry began to cry, as if he understood how severely he would suffer for his sister's defeat.

"All right," Greta said sullenly. "You win. . . . Lemme up."

I got off her prone body, and she rose to her feet. We stared at one another in silence. There was something enigmatic in Greta's face, an expression that encompassed more than defeat, as if she had suddenly recognized me as a male and as a force.

The encounter had been a strange one for me as well, highlighting the differences between boy and girl I had accepted so casually to that time. I recalled the feel of Greta's body supine under me, her thighs squirming beneath my legs, my chest mashed against her chest so I felt the small mounds of her budding breasts.

That contest and victory marked a change in me. It was as if a part of my body I had not really focused on before was suddenly clamoring for my attention. By unspoken agreement, Greta and I did not wrestle again. But I was conscious, sometimes, of her watching me. And our games took on a different mood and excitement for me, spawned by a flash of Greta's bare thighs or a glimpse of the white cotton panties she wore under her short frock.

I also rediscovered the magazine rack in the small gas station store located on the highway about a mile from our cottage. The rack was filled with material that had previously interested me only because of the comic books and pulp stories. But for the first time that summer, I noticed among the magazines one called *Spicy Fun* that, when I leafed through it, revealed stunning photographs of naked women adorned with a profusion of breasts and thighs that pulverized me. Their body parts were not Greta's spare titties or the skinny legs of my sister but the great nippled melons and white satiny thighs of full-bodied women. I no longer had to be content with stealing furtive peeks under her dress as Greta climbed a tree. In the magazine, everything was exposed. Nor was there reason to reproach myself or feel guilty for gawking, because the flirtatious, teasing expressions on the faces of the naked beauties suggested that they invited and approved of my fervid stares.

The gas station owner would have been outraged (and might even have told my father) if I had tried to buy a copy, so I would spend an hour lingering over my Coke, waiting for those intervals when a car on the highway pulled up to the gas pump. When the owner left the store to pump gas, I would fly to the rack and leaf deftly through the beguiling magazine. Swiftly and ardently I memorized every slope and globe, every curve and crescent, to be recalled at my leisure later on.

In the sanctuary of my bed at night, my sinful hand clutching that unquiet appendage, I drew on my memory of the photographs in the magazine, and in a worn, well-stained washcloth I kept hidden under the mattress, I achieved my fevered release. Afterward, I slept the tranquil sleep of a liberated male.

Near the end of August, a mother and her daughter who were friends of Mrs. Schroeder's came to spend a week with her. The mother, Mrs. Rivers, was a tall, somber-faced woman who wore thick-lensed glasses that made her eyes appear ready to pop out of her head. It was hard to imagine that she could have a daughter like Christina.

Christina was twenty years old, a small, slender girl who, when she stood beside me, made me feel bigger than I really was. She had long, golden hair that she gathered into a pearl clasp from which it cascaded in a silky pony's mane down her back. When she walked across the room, her golden tresses frolicked in her wake.

Below the shimmering crown of her hair, she had large, blue eyes, a petite nose, and tiny ears. She had a way of bringing out her tongue to moisten her shapely lips that made my breath lock in my throat. But it was her smile that most illuminated and enhanced her beauty. When she smiled at me for the first time, I felt as if I were immersed in sunlight instead of standing in the shadowed cottage.

Despite the difference in our ages, Christina joined our games with the fervor and delight of a child, scampering with us through the woods, racing alongside us in the pastures, even climbing the limbs of trees. It was as if she were abandoning her adulthood and embracing once again some childhood world she remembered.

Her loveliness seemed to me more glorious than that of any of the women I had seen in the magazine. Indeed, all that week of Christina's visit, I never went to the magazine rack at the store. I had no need of the spurious, inanimate beauty of photographs when I had a flesh and blood nymph before me instead.

Christina's beauty was confirmed for me in a dialogue I heard between her mother, my mother, and Mrs. Schroeder, who were all sitting on our screen porch. I had returned to the cottage to pick up a soft drink. They did not hear me enter, and I stood in the kitchen, hidden from view, listening to them speak about Christina.

"She's such a pretty girl," my mother said. "I can understand why men chase her."

"You have no idea," Mrs. Rivers said dolefully. "They won't leave the poor girl alone. Flowers, cards, and boxes of candy come to our house almost every day. They just won't leave her alone, and I worry myself sick about her."

"Does she enjoy all the attention?" Mrs. Schroeder asked. "Sometimes it turns a young girl's head."

"She doesn't enjoy it!" Mrs. Rivers said brusquely. "How can she enjoy it when they never give her a minute's rest?"

"A girl as pretty as she is can get into trouble," my mother said, then quickly added, "not through any fault of her own, of course, but because they won't leave her alone."

"She's a good girl and she tries to do what's right," Mrs. Rivers said. "That's why I was glad to get her away from the city for a little while." A deep sigh resonated from within her body. "You know how filthy men can be."

In the ominous silence that followed, as I slipped quietly away, I ruminated on how filthy men could be. That night in bed I brooded and fumed over the image of Christina fleeing before a horde of leering, rapacious males.

All week long Christina continued to play with us, bare-legged and barefooted as we were, careless as we were careless in the way we hurled ourselves around. I tried valiantly to conceal how much she excited and enthralled me. Glimpsing Christina's legs was a tantalizing feast for my eyes. And the sight of her lightly covered breasts heaving with exertion after running caused my head to whirl.

Late one afternoon, when the setting sun cast a lustrous glow across the earth, we were all sitting beneath the ghost tree. When it was time to leave and we rose, a gust of vagrant wind caught the hem of Christina's frock and whipped it to her waist. I was nearly blinded by the sight of her slender bare legs and the briefest, pinkest silk panties I had ever seen. That vision lasted only a second, but I will never forget how my heartbeat quickened. Then I saw Greta watching me and, for an instant, was shocked at the fury I saw glowing in her eyes.

Near the end of that week, Mrs. Schroeder decided to drive into Waukegan to shop. Mrs. Rivers, Jerry and Greta, and my mother and sister drove with her. There wasn't room for all of us, so Christina volunteered to stay behind. I quickly resolved to stay as well, telling my mother I wanted to read instead. For the first time all week, Christina and I were left alone. After the others had driven off, I suggested a boat ride around the channel, and Christina agreed. We walked down to the pier, and I helped her into the rowboat. She sat in the stern facing me while I shattered the water with the wooden oars, eager to display my rowing skill and strength. Meanwhile, my fevered eyes were drawn, like a moth to the flame, to her bare thighs visible under her dress. In an effort to conceal my ardent glances, I glared at my oars, stared up at the sky, frowned and whistled.

I need not have worried, because after a while Christina seemed not to know I was there. She leaned languidly back on her seat, one delicate hand trailing in the water, her fingers caressing lilies the boat passed. There was so sad and thoughtful a look on her face in that moment that I barely restrained myself from heaving aside the oars and rushing to embrace and console her.

We moored the boat and walked through the woods to the old cemetery. Although I had played among the graves for years, I had never paid attention to the names on the faded stone tablets. As we entered the enclosure, Christina bent to read them.

"'Miriam Abbot, born February 13, 1804, died February 23, 1884,'" Christina said softly. "She lived a long, long life, but the dates tell nothing of whether it was a sad or happy life."

She walked slowly past cracked stone markers lying flat on the grass, and I followed her. Close by, half-hidden in the weeds, a squirrel watched us warily. Christina paused before another stone.

"'Daniel Walden, born without a birth date as a slave in Virginia. He escaped to Illinois and lived by the name of Charles Valentine until his death, January 8, 1856.'" She reached out to gently touch the weathered stone. "He died just a few years before the Civil War was fought to free men like him," she said.

The fading light of late afternoon shadowed the edges of the cemetery. On the horizon, the descending sun cast a crimson glow across Christina's cheeks. A bird passed overhead, trailing a shrill, short cry. For the first time, I understood that the graves beneath the tablets and markers held men and women who had once lived.

"Oh, Alex, look at this one!" Christina said, and I bent beside her over another grave.

"'Charles Rawlins MacIver,'" Christina read. "'Hanged in accordance with the law for the murder of his sweetheart. This tablet placed here by his mother who forgives him and prays God forgives him too.'"

Christina stared at the grave.

"Did he kill his sweetheart because he loved her or hated her?" she asked softly. "And think how his poor mother must have grieved to see her own son hanged."

She moved to another grave.

"'In memory of Isabella H. daughter of William and Matilda Walker, who died May 30, 1842, aged 2 years and four months. Also James D. who died December 24, 1843, aged 10 days. Sleep on sweet babes and take your rest.'"

Christina turned to me, her cheeks wet with tears.

"The poor things died so young," she said sadly. "They were only babies, and they died before they had a chance to live."

She stared down at the stone for a long time, and I hardly dared to breathe because I didn't want to disturb her.

Finally, she turned and walked over to me. She gently clasped my hand so that with fingers entwined we walked from the cemetery. I realized in that tender moment how much I loved her.

So many years have passed since that thirteenth summer of my life. I have traveled the world, looked into the faces of numerous men and women, been spectator and participant through sorrows and joys. I witnessed the decline and death of my parents. I have loved a few women, been married twice, and have sons and a daughter and beloved grandchildren. As one of the old letter writers who scrolled carefully in ink would say, "I am here, at the end of my sheet."

As I've grown older, with the passage of time many early memories have faded. But that last summer we spent at the lake has not blurred or dissolved in my mind. I can still see the cottage and the pasture, old man Murray's cows, the ghost tree and the woods. And I remember with the greatest clarity the days Christina spent with us: the way she ran and played like a child beside us, how she looked reclining in the boat, her fingers caressing lilies in the water. And I also recall with a curious ache in my heart the old cemetery where Christina first helped me understand the dualities of love and death.

I never saw Christina again after that summer and never knew what happened to her. Mrs. Schroeder died many years ago, Jerry moved overseas, and Greta married and had several children and lived, the last I'd heard, somewhere in California. Then, out of the blue, one Christmas I got a card from Greta. I sent her a New Year's card in return and asked if she knew what had happened to Christina. Some weeks later Greta wrote me a note back saying she couldn't remember anyone named Christina coming to visit her mother that summer.

How strange that she cannot remember what I can never forget.

Chicago's Greek Town is one of the finest—if not the finest—in the United States, with a dozen restaurants lining several blocks along South Halsted Street. People often ask me which is my favorite, but I would be hard-pressed to name fewer than five or six I patronize and enjoy.

While eating lunches and dinners, I have often observed the young waiters, many newly arrived from Greece, handsome, dark-haired youths whose dreams have nothing to do with the food they serve. I have listened to their caustic, often comic exchanges with one another and have tried to convey some of that banter in this story.

My wife believes that the owner's daughter in the story, a modest Greek girl, would not have exposed herself so brazenly to any young man. But who am I to decide what a young girl would or would not do when she finds herself alone with a young man who obviously idolizes her?

Rites of Passage

FOR THE FIRST TWENTY YEARS OF HIS LIFE, the village of Elanda in the mountains of central Greece composed the boundaries of Panos's life. He had been trying to escape from the age of fifteen, but since his father was dead, his mother and younger sister needed his help. There was also the almost impossible task of gathering money for the fare to leave. And even if one had the fare, immigration to the United States had become more difficult because of stricter laws on entering the country.

That unhappy situation was the same in all the villages of their region. Some of the young men who did manage to leave had emigrated to Germany. They wrote letters home relating how unhappy they were working as menials among German natives who held them in contempt.

Another reason for Panos to leave was that in another country, he might find a job and send money home to help his family. The only work available to him in the village came in the fields at sowing and harvest time or in tending a small flock of scrawny goats on the slope of the mountain. From that vantage point, Panos could see the tour buses in the valley below on their way to Delphi and the Gulf of Corinth. If it were not for their small vegetable garden, a few chickens, and a goat of their own, Panos and his mother and sister wouldn't have been able to afford to eat.

Life in the village had become intolerable. In addition to the lack of work, his greatest burden was boredom. In the evenings, Panos had to choose between spending his time in the small village hall, which had the only small black and white television set in the village (he had seen episodes of *I Love Lucy* and *Bonanza* a score of times), or joining the older men in the *kafeneion*, who spent their days and nights smoking and drinking rank black coffee, telling and retelling stories of their bravery in battle against the Italians, the Germans, the Communists. Each time Panos entered the kafeneion, he was repelled by the smells of waste and decay in the room that was as drab as a tomb. Over the tables dangled strips of flypaper clotted with snared flies.

That hopelessness was reflected even in the rituals of village courtship. Families arranged marriages that the young men and young women accepted with resignation. Love was rare because there were no longer any suitable girls in the village. Bleakness and hopelessness had drained their complexions of color, slumped their shoulders, saddened their eyes. They were less able than the young men to escape, and if they did manage to marry, their fate was to bear children and join the cluster of weary, older women in black dresses with black shawls over their heads.

The plight of the young men was the same in all the villages of Panos's region. Some who could not bear to wait any longer left for the ports of Patras or Piraeus in the hope of signing on as porters or cabin boys on the freighters, only so they could jump ship in the harbors of American ports. A few drowned and others were caught and sent back to Greece.

Yet, despite the rigors and dangers of the journey, the dream of escape and making one's fortune was revitalized by the occasional return of a former villager who had become rich and successful in America. Word would spread through the mountains, and people would gather from miles around to greet him. He would generally arrive for a brief stay in a big car with a bulging wallet and a fashionable Athenian girl on his arm. For a little while, everyone seethed with excitement until the wealthy Greek American left again for Athens and America. The villages would then recede again into the dusty torpor of their days and nights.

Panos's feelings of hopelessness and a growing despair were echoed by the village schoolteacher, Apostolos Zervas, a scrawny, wasted little man with teeth yellowed from incessant smoking. Because he was the best-educated man in the village, villagers called him "Little Aristotle." Although he urged all the young men to escape, he showed a special affection for Panos and gave him his first rudimentary lessons in English so the young man would "be ready" when his chance came.

"You're a bright boy, Panaki," Little Aristotle told him, "but your brightness will tarnish here unless you get away as soon as you can! You see what happens to even the dogs in our village? They become so depressed that when cats or rabbits scurry by them, they haven't the will or spirit to bark or chase! Listen to me and get out!"

An opportunity for Panos to escape presented itself in the spring of that year when a letter came from Plato Lagounis, a former villager who had become a successful restaurateur in America, saying he'd sponsor four more of the young men from the village. In past years he had sponsored a half dozen youths, bringing them to America to work in his restaurant.

His letter caused great excitement among the young men. Since there were twenty more than the four Mr. Lagounis was willing to sponsor who were anxious to leave, it was decided by the village elders that a lottery, under the supervision of Little Aristotle, would select the winners. When the names of the lucky youths were announced, Panos was one of the four. He suspected that his teacher had contrived to select him.

The aging village priest, Father Kostas, held a special service in the little stone church for the boys who were going to leave. All the villagers gathered in the church, thick with the smells of candles and incense. Father Kostas gave communion to each of the young men. As the priest bent to insert the tiny spoon with wine into Panos's mouth, Panos noticed the worn and threadbare sleeves of the old priest's robe and his gray beard flecked with crumbs of food from his dinner the night before.

A few days later, Panos bid a tearful farewell to his sister and mother, who gave him two small jars of grape and peach preserves and a few extra drachmas she had been saving for years. The entire village gathered to see the four young men off as they mounted the cart and rode down the mountain to the town of Tripoli, where they would catch the bus that would take them to the airport near Athens. Three days after leaving the village and following a flight of less than a dozen hours, Panos arrived in the city of Chicago, the teeming metropolis he had seen before only on television. A representative of Mr. Lagounis met the four young men at the airport, helping them through immigration and afterward driving them to the small rooming house where they would live. The following morning, he told them, he'd pick them up at dawn so they could begin their work in the restaurant.

Lying in his small room that first night, weary from his journey and yet, due to his excitement, unable to sleep, Panos listened to the sounds of the city: the noise of cars and horns and, from time to time, a siren wailing across the night. America, America, he whispered the word over and over again. It was the last thing he remembered before he fell into a heavy, exhausted sleep.

The Apollo, one of the larger Greek restaurants on Halsted Street, was governed by a strict hierarchy of prestige and power that began with Mr. Lagounis, who ruled like a monarch. After him came the principal chef, Mr. Kaloyannis. Then there were the two headwaiters, Sotiris and Zogas. Sotiris was quick-witted and quick-tongued, and Zogas had a muscular build and brawny arms. If a caustic tongue-lashing by Sotiris didn't teach a new employee his place, he was threatened with a visit to the alley by Zogas, who promised to give the miscreant "a sturdy kick in the ass!"

After these two headwaiters came the grill cooks and about twenty-five waiters. The level below cooks and waiters was occupied by the busboys and the dishwashers. Although there were washing machines in the kitchen, the great, greasy pots in which much of the food was cooked still had to be scoured and cleaned by hand.

During his first six months in the restaurant, Panos worked as a busboy, one of the dumb brutes whose task was to gather the stained glasses and soiled plates. Panos moved among the tables with his trays as if he were a ghost, at the beck and call of every waiter. If he did not clear their tables quickly enough, he was treated to a hissed curse. His only exchange with the customers came when one would ask him for water or an extra napkin, but he knew they never really saw him. He was as much a part of the furniture as the tables, chairs, and murals of Greece that decorated the walls.

Panos was resolved to better himself, and three times a week he went to an English language class to improve the rudimentary English he had learned from his teacher in the village. As a result of his study, he was promoted to the position of waiter.

Mr. Lagounis lectured Panos gravely on the responsibilities his new position entailed.

"You will now deal directly with the public," he told him. "How courteously and how quickly you respond to their wishes will determine whether they return again. Even more important, it will help fashion their impression of that vaunted Greek hospitality we Greeks call *filotimo*. So remember, Panos, all the hallowed legacy of Greek *filotimo* rests now on your shoulders. Don't betray Greece and the Apollo by letting us down!"

After joining the ranks of waiters, Panos came to understand there were sublevels of prestige among them as well. After Sotiris and Zogas, the group was led by the waiters from Athens, who boasted of the marvels of that cosmopolitan city, Syntagma Square and Queen Sophia Avenue, the Acropolis and the Hilton. They looked on the youths from the villages with derision and called them "bumpkins" and "hicks."

Once he had gained his position as a waiter, Panos kept his mouth shut and tried to do his work quickly and efficiently. The Apollo did a thriving business seven days a week, and the waiters who hustled made good tips. After paying for his lodging in a nearby rooming house, Panos was able to send most of his money to his mother and sister in his village.

Most of the restaurant patrons were tourists visiting Chicago, students from the nearby campus of the University of Illinois, and a handful of Greek Americans. The weekend nights were the busiest with the restaurant tables packed and a line of people waiting to be seated. The waiters and busboys dashed back and forth among the patrons who were fat or thin, homely or comely, laughing, eating, gorging, swilling. And, rising above the din of voices and clatter of utensils, was the rousing chant of a waiter crying "Oppaaa!" as he lit the trays of *saganaki* he carried in a row on his arm.

From the crowded restaurant area, the waiters hurried in and out of the organized bedlam of the kitchen where the minor cooks, generally older men whose cheeks had become as baked and dark as the fare they prepared, responded to their orders. This phalanx of waiters and cooks was constantly at war, unleashing upon each other a cacophony of curses.

"A moron has more sense than you!"

"Your birth, Gorgios, must have given your mother a stroke!"

"Back home I had a crippled jackass who moved faster than you!"

"I asked for lamb with artichokes, not green beans!"

"Son of a goat!"

"Brother of a pig!"

The contentious, bickering voices fell silent only when the ominous figure of Mr. Lagounis entered the kitchen. He was a burly man with a mottled complexion and the thick neck of a bull. His burning, always angry gaze lashed the kitchen like a whip.

"Who is eager to leave?" his harsh voice cracked across the steam-filled room. "Who wants to work elsewhere? Tell me now so I don't waste any time before sending you on your way!"

After one of his fleeting visits to the kitchen, the pace of all labor increased. Cooks worked faster. Waiters moved more quickly. Even the busboys carried their heavy trays of dishes with greater energy.

At the beginning of his second year at the Apollo, Panos became aware of how much he disliked working in the restaurant. His stomach revolted at the assorted smells of food. He became repelled by the sight of people eating, the hollow and never-ending shouts of 'Oppaaa!," the bullying and hostility of Sotiris and Zogas, the endless wrangling between waiters and cooks, the stern admonitions of Mr. Lagounis.

With a number of the other young waiters he enrolled in accounting courses at the nearby University of Illinois Circle Campus. He managed to attend his weekly class, but after working ten-hour shifts, he couldn't muster the alertness to study and his grades suffered. He considered finding another job that would allow him more free time and also more energy for school, but he was apprehensive about leaving the familiar environment of the restaurant and to mingle with strangers. He dropped his courses and vowed to make another effort the following year.

At the end of Panos's second year as a waiter, an event took place in the restaurant that, at a single stroke, united the contentious cooks, waiters, busboys, and dishwashers. That astonishing compatibility was achieved by the arrival at the Apollo of Sofoula, the twenty-year-old daughter of Mr. Lagounis.

Sofoula Lagounis was slender-bodied with long, raven-shaded hair she wore to her shoulders. Her complexion was a rich blending of cream and olive, her eyes large, luminous, and dark. She generally wore a white blouse and dark skirt, and that modest attire did more to accentuate her attractiveness than bolder clothing worn by many of the girls who came into the Apollo. On those occasions when her full, sensual lips curled in a faint smile, the area around her seemed bathed in sunlight.

The afternoon she first appeared, Panos shared in the admiration and awe with every other man, whether young or old, who first saw her. In the locker room the young waiters rolled their eyes and slapped their heads.

"Helen of Troy would have been jealous!"

"When she first walked in, I nearly dropped the damn tray with three orders of lamb chops! Lagounis would have killed me!"

"Her eyes could scar a man's heart!"

"Her lips glisten like jewels!"

Panos kept his admiration to himself but found it hard to understand how such a craggy, hard-hearted, and snarling man could have helped produce such a flower.

Sofoula did not mingle in the restaurant among the jostling, pushing crowds but remained isolated behind the register, seated on a high stool. From that island, shielded by a cigar counter, she handled the cash and credit cards from the customers and the waiters. In her presence, patrons and employees were all but rendered mute before her dazzling beauty.

However much they admired Sofoula, the men who worked at the Apollo remained guarded and reserved in her presence. That was because of the fierce and protective vigilance Mr. Lagounis mustered around his daughter. He watched the waiters bring her credit cards, wary of anything remotely indicating flirtatiousness. The waiters didn't dare smile at Sofoula for fear Mr. Lagounis might deem the smile impertinent. If a waiter lingered too long in the monetary exchange with Sofoula, Mr. Lagounis might order the culprit into the kitchen and deliver a tongue-lashing to him. There was even a rumor of a large black revolver—although no one had ever seen it—that Mr. Lagounis kept locked in a drawer of his desk in his office, a revolver he had vowed to use against any scoundrel insolent and foolhardy enough to say or do anything he found offensive toward his daughter.

Panos was as respectful toward Sofoula as the rest of the waiters at the Apollo. But away from the restaurant, in his fervid imaginings, his erotic fantasies would have earned him all six bullets from her father's gun.

He even allowed himself the audacious illusion that Sofoula might find him pleasing to look at. Despite his shyness, he felt he was one of the better-looking young waiters. He stood slightly above average height with dark, curly hair, dark eyes, and a strongly chiseled nose and jaw. The girls who came into the restaurant sometimes looked at him boldly. He would have liked to have asked one of them out, but he was painfully shy and wouldn't have known how or where to begin. He had to be satisfied with the indecent fantasies (mostly about Sofoula) that provided him a measure of release before he fell into wearied sleep.

Spring passed into summer, and the city was caught in the clutches of a wrenching heat. Despite the air conditioning at the Apollo, the restaurant air was heavy and humid. The waiters worked with sweat-stained shirts glued to their backs and served the customers who were dressed in T-shirts, shorts, and sandals. That curtailment of clothing also applied to Sofoula, who changed from blouse and skirt into light, sleeveless, diaphanous frocks that fell in loose folds about her slender body. When Panos carried her a credit card for a check, he had to rip his gaze away from the sheen of sweat glistening across her throat and bare shoulders.

Sometimes when he was a safe distance from her, Panos found himself thinking that she could not be happy sitting in the same spot, hour after hour, unable to move around the restaurant. For a trembling moment, despite her beauty, he found himself pitying her.

There was a night that summer when Panos incurred the wrath of Sotiris after he'd taken the blame for something a helpless busboy had done. Panos's punishment was to spend the following few days after his shift ended unpacking cans of produce in the storeroom off the loading dock in the back of the kitchen. For the next three nights, Panos worked uncrating the produce from the stacks of boxes, which took him near the time the restaurant closed.

On the last night Panos spent uncrating and stacking, the kitchen empty except for a cook scraping the grills and a dishwasher scouring the last of the pots, he heard someone entering the storeroom. When he looked up, he was astonished to see Sofoula.

They stood a few feet apart in the shadowed storeroom. Panos couldn't see her face clearly in the dark alcove, but he still felt the searing power of her eyes.

"Good evening, Miss Sofoula." He felt his words pull against a tightness in his throat.

"My father had to go on an errand," she said. "I'm waiting for him to pick me up."

In the strained silence that followed, he struggled to find something appropriate and respectful to say. He felt a twinge of fear when he considered her father walking in and finding them together.

"I think Sotiris was unfair," she said. "What Vasili did wasn't your fault. But you acted nobly and took the blame."

"It wasn't anything special," Panos said in a low voice. He felt the sweat on his palms and on his forehead. From the kitchen beyond he could hear the voices of the dishwasher and cook.

"I have seen you looking at me," Sofoula said, her voice low and intense.

Panos was seized by a flare of panic, a feeling that he might have offended her and she'd tell her father. As if she sensed his distress, she spoke again quickly.

"I don't mind," she said. "You're different than the others. You look at me in a different way." She paused. "Do you think I'm pretty?"

He wanted to tell her how weak and inadequate a word "pretty" was to describe her loveliness, but he couldn't muster the courage.

"Tell me!" and there was a sudden urgency in her voice. "Tell me you think I'm pretty."

As Panos struggled for the courage to tell her what he felt, he wished he had the verbal facility of Sotiris.

"You are beautiful," he said, his voice almost a whisper. "The most beautiful girl I have ever seen."

She let out her breath in a tremulous sigh. He wondered suddenly if that was the first time she had heard a man speak those words.

"I think you're handsome too, Panos," she said. "And the way you look at me, so sweetly, so shyly. Not the way those louts from Athens look at me."

He was shaken by her praise.

"Do you like me?" she asked.

"Of course! Yes!" He tried not to stammer.

"Do you love me?"

He had never dared consider so brazen a thought.

"Don't be afraid," she said. "I won't tell anyone."

He threw caution and restraint to the winds.

"If your father heard me, I know he'd shoot me," Panos said, "but I don't care, Sofoula, because I do love you!" He was pleased at the sound of the words. "I love you!"

She looked quickly back toward the kitchen and then moved a step closer.

"Because you love me," she said, and her voice trembled, "I'll show you what no other man has ever seen before"—her hand rose to the collar of her dress, her fingers fumbling at the buttons—"and what no man will ever see again until I marry."

She loosened several buttons and pulled the fabric of her dress aside. He saw the mounds of her breasts cradled in a wispy band of silk. Then she tugged the silken band loose so her breasts emerged, naked and free.

The only female breasts he had ever seen were the pendulous boobs of old Kyra Xanthippe when he saw her bathing at the stream and the puny teats of his sister. He had never imagined that breasts as lovely as Sofoula's might exist.

They were not large, and even in the shadows, he saw a tiny network of purple veins beneath the smoothness of her skin. But it was their astonishing symmetry that filled him with awe, each shapely sphere rising to a small crest adorned with a perfectly shaped nipple. He had a sudden vision of lush white grapes absorbing the crimson reflection of the sun.

Then, as if suddenly conscious of how brazen her revelation had been, she quickly buttoned her dress.

"You'll never tell anyone, will you?" her voice was shaken.

"Never!" his own voice trembled. "I swear, Sofoula, on my mother's life!"

With a final, fleeting look, she turned then and quickly left the storeroom. He stood there without moving for several minutes, fearing to walk out of the shadows because he thought that anyone seeing him would detect the image of Sofoula's breasts graven on his cheeks and in his eyes.

Back in his room that night he lay across his bed, trying to recall in painstaking detail every second that had transpired between them, what Sofoula and he had said. And all the words were simply a prelude to the stunning moment when she had showed him her breasts.

For the following week, Panos worked with an inner turmoil. Each time he had to come to the register with a check, he tried to avert his eyes from Sofoula for fear she might think him too bold. When he did steal a fleeting glance at her, he saw that she averted her eyes, as well.

But as he watched Sofoula furtively from vantage points across the restaurant, Panos saw what he hadn't seen before: how stiffly and unhappily she sat on her stool, reflecting the image of someone imprisoned, repressed, unable to reveal her true emotions.

For a few irrational hours he considered speaking to Mr. Lagounis, confessing that he loved Sofoula and asking to be allowed to court her. He realized quickly that would be a mistake. The owner of the Apollo had more grandiose plans for his daughter than having her wooed by a lowly waiter.

But all that week he could not resist a feeling of jubilation. Among the two dozen young waiters, including the eloquent Sotiris and the muscular Zogas, Sofoula had chosen him. He felt as if she had sensed his uniqueness, understood he was foreordained for some exceptional destiny. He decided he could not disappoint her by remaining a waiter at the Apollo. He had to go out into the world and make his fortune.

On Friday of that week, he told Mr. Lagounis he was leaving.

"Do you have another job?"

"No," Panos said.

Mr. Lagounis stared at him sharply.

"Do you have money saved?"

"I send almost all I make home to my mother and sister."

"You're crazy . . . *trellos*!" Mr. Lagounis said brusquely. "Maybe it's a disease you've picked up here in America! You should see a doctor!"

But he wasn't crazy and he didn't need a doctor. He felt confident that he'd make his way and find another position where he wouldn't be at the beck and call of anyone with a few dollars for a plate of gyros and a Greek salad. He would never have to flame the platters of *saganaki* and cry the foolish "Oppaaa!" again.

He worked the weekend, and on Sunday evening, without having to face Sofoula, who didn't work that day, he said good-bye to all the waiters, cooks, and busboys. Mr. Lagounis gave him his final week's wages, shaking his head and muttering, "*Trellos . . . trellos . . .*"

With a final jaunty wave of farewell, Panos strode briskly to the door. He opened it and, without a trace of hesitation or fear, walked out into the teeming city to begin his new life.

There may be readers who object to this story and feel the ending unrealistic. They may feel life has enough perplexities without introducing an element of the supernatural. Yet the story also speaks about our longing to believe that something survives our mortal bodies even if reason dictates otherwise. Let's remember for a moment that after Hamlet has talked with his father's ghost, he relates the experience to his friend, Horatio.

> HORATIO:
> O day and night, but this is wondrous strange!
> HAMLET:
> And therefore as a stranger give it welcome.
> There are more things in heaven and earth, Horatio,
> Than are dreamt of in your philosophy.

All I am asking each reader now to do is to make the dishwasher's tale welcome.

A Dishwasher's Tale

THERE ARE NO HEROES. THERE ARE ONLY DESPERATE MEN, and afterward, the deluded poets sing of their exploits. In the same way, there is no supernatural, no mystery beyond the reality of the wretched days and nights we live. A lifetime of hate, contempt, mistrust, prejudice—the hallmarks of contemporary life—is more than enough. Only an imbecile would ask for more time, and his stupidity wouldn't know what to do with eternity anyway.

You might think it strange that a dishwasher should talk this way, but there isn't any rule that says a dishwasher must be ignorant. For example, I, Nikos Poneros, in my seventieth year, an extensive reader and amateur philosopher, long ago chose dishwashing as a profession.

Earlier in my life I was married to a shrew, betrayed in business by a partner, deceived by a priest, lied to by a doctor. These experiences fashioned my philosophy that life is an ordeal one must get through as quickly as possible. I also believe, with Epicurus, that there is nothing but oblivion after death and nothing dreadful any longer in life for a man who understands that there is nothing terrible in not living.

To prove my scorn of wealth, power, and fame and to enhance my immunity to the seductive wiles of blonde and dark women, I chose the most menial of professions. Others may prattle about the simple life, but I live it daily. Similes and metaphors are unnecessary. My life is plain, factual description without any effort at ornamentation. I repeat, I am a dishwasher.

Consistent with my general philosophy, although I am of Greek ancestry, I remain unaffected by the virus of adulation for the revered past that prevails among many of my fellow Greeks. There are a few exceptions, such as the aforementioned Epicurus and the dramatist Sophocles when he wrote, "Never to have lived is best." But for the most part, I count it little reason for pride that a senile octogenarian named Socrates got poisoned and a bellicose clod named Odysseus got lost. Nor do I have any desire to visit a land strewn with headless statues and ruined temples.

What remains essential for any life, however simple it may be, is friendship. Life without a friend is death without a witness. My closest friend is Spiros Karras, who sells hot dogs from a wagon, an occupation only a level or two above my own. He is also Greek, a decent old man but one full of illusions. I don't say it to malign him but because it is true.

One afternoon in August, after I finished my dishwashing shift at the Olympia restaurant, I walked a few blocks north to Harrison Street to sit for a while with Spiros beside his wagon. He had once owned the shabby Plaka lunchroom in the middle of the block but, like that idiot Lear, had given it away to his sons, a pair of matched louts. To show their gratitude, they had put their father on the street with the hot dog wagon to get him out of the way.

While the sons were big, stocky, and surly, Spiros was slight of build and usually temperate in manner. In contrast to my own bald head, he had thick white hair above a face totally lacking in guile. He was a fervent believer in all the trappings of myth and an avid teller of stories. The man had the gift of taking the most mundane experiences and, by his passion and faith, recasting them as high adventures. Listening to him ramble about the exploits of the old heroes could be entertaining, but from time to time I felt it sensible to reattach him to reality.

"What adventure do you wish to hear today, Nikos?" Spiro asked me as we sat together on the street. "Shall it be Jason braving the wrath of the dragon to seize the Golden Fleece, or Prometheus stealing fire from the gods for the human race?"

"Surprise me, Spiros," I said. That was unlikely because I had heard the old man's fairy tales numerous times.

Before he could begin, a burly, sweating customer in shorts paused at the wagon and asked for a hot dog. Spiros rose stiffly to his feet and slowly retrieved a bun from the steamer. He added the hot dog and turned to the condiments, which he invariably mixed up.

"I didn't want no onions," the customer said.

"No onions," Spiros repeated. He held the hot dog limply in a napkin and tried to shake off the onions until he noticed the man glaring at him. Spiros handed the hot dog to me and made another one for the customer.

"You forgot the mustard," the man snapped.

Spiros added a glob of mustard. After paying him, the customer walked off muttering. Spiros put the change in his cash box and sat down again on his stool.

"Who was the greatest warrior in the Greek armies that besieged Troy?" he asked.

"Achilles," I said.

"Who was the beloved friend of Achilles?" he pressed on. "By killing him in battle, Hector ordained his own death."

"Patroclus," I replied crisply. "He wasn't as great as Hector or Achilles, a sort of designated hitter when the big fellows weren't around."

"Who was the most beautiful of women, the queen who watched armies clash in battle for her favor?"

Growing impatient, I said, "The beautiful Helen Kowalski from Bridgeport."

Spiros's indignation was deflected when a man and woman stopped for hot dogs. The old man rose again and fumbled at the tray. He prepared a hot dog that he handed to the woman and then made one for the man.

"I didn't want relish," the man said.

Spiros stared at him numbly.

"He said he didn't want relish," I repeated.

"I heard!" Spiros said peevishly. "Do you think I am deaf?" He made the man another hot dog and handed the one saturated with relish to me. I was eating too many hot dogs but took it to avoid offending him.

Spiros sat back on his stool. Beneath the rim of his cap, his forehead and cheeks were beaded with sweat. A few cars rumbled along the street.

"Do you remember where we left off in the *Iliad*?" Spiros asked, his eyes gleaming in the pale circles of his face. Without waiting for my answer, he continued. "Hector had killed Patroclus, the beloved friend of Achilles. In his grief and rage, Achilles appears before the Trojan walls, his armor flaming in the sun, and challenges Hector to a battle to the death. At first, Hector fears to fight the great Greek warrior. But the treacherous gods instilled in him the will and courage to accept the challenge."

He paused in his story and looked sharply at me.

"What's wrong with you?" he asked. "I am relating this epic encounter and you sit there gloomy as a mourner . . ."

"That last hot dog is not resting easy in my stomach."

The old man shrugged off my complaint.

"Hector and Achilles begin to battle fiercely," Spiros said, "slashing and stabbing at one another, neither warrior able to gain an advantage." The old man's lip curled disdainfully. "But the fickle gods couldn't abide a fair fight. Athena, that most perverse of goddesses, tricks Hector into believing that if he continues fighting, he will be victorious."

Although I had heard the story many times, I marveled at how Spiros always told it as if he were relating it for the first time.

"Finally, his throat pierced by Achilles' spear, Hector falls mortally wounded." Spiros's voice grew low and sorrowful. "With his dying breath, Hector pleads with Achilles not to cast his body to the dogs but to allow him a warrior's burial. Achilles is too full of rage to listen, and he strips the dying Hector of his armor . . ."

As the late afternoon sun slipped behind the skyline of the city, the shadows around us grew longer. A few passing autos turned on lights that cast fleeting beams across Spiros's wagon. Spiros paused once more and glared at me. "Are you listening?"

"I'm listening," I said. "A thrilling fairy tale."

"Fairy tale?" the old man cried. "How many times do I have to tell you this is no story but the truth!"

We had engaged in this same argument many times.

"You were there, of course!" I couldn't resist the barb. "You peddled hot dogs from a wagon outside the Trojan walls. Achilles liked his without mustard but with plenty of onions."

"How can a cynic like you be descended from our noble heritage?" the old man cried.

"I was smarter before I started eating your hot dogs."

He shook his head in disgust. "Standing over your dish tub all day has soured you on life!"

I had soured on life long before I began washing dishes.

"You'd be surprised at the perspective one gets over a dish tub," I said brusquely. "Politicians, philosophers, and generals assume their proper place. Your chums Achilles and Hector were also men who soiled their plates."

"You are an earthbound creature!" Spiros fumed. "You don't allow yourself to take wing and dream!"

I stared into his impassioned face and realized how fond I was of the misguided old man. I softened my tone.

"All right," I said. "Go on with your tale. Perhaps it is the suspense and not the hot dog that has curdled my stomach."

Sulking slightly, Spiros began again.

"Achilles ties the dying Hector to the back of his chariot!" The old man's face and voice reflected his anguish. "Then he drags the Trojan hero's body three times around the walls of the city, while the blood streaming from Hector's wounds inflames the wild dogs which run barking behind them. And on the city walls, the Trojan king, Priam, wails in sorrow at this terrible defilement of the body of his son . . ."

Neither of us saw Spiros's son, Leontis, come from the lunchroom in his soiled apron, a scowl on his pustule-blemished face. He stood with his hands on his hips, glaring down at the old man.

"Jesus Christ, Pa!" he said. "You sit here in the shadows where no one can see you! What the hell's the matter with you? Move the damn wagon under the streetlight!"

The old man looked nervously at his son and rose slowly and pushed the wagon beneath the light.

"What the hell you always hanging around for?" Leontis asked me.

The churlish oaf made me grateful I had never had children.

"I'm with the city health department," I said brusquely. "I'm making a sanitary survey of pushcarts. Next week I'll start on lunchrooms."

"A wise guy," he sneered.

"No one would ever mistake you for one," I said scornfully.

As if he thought I needed help, Spiros turned back to defend me.

"Nikos is my friend," he said.

Leontis looked at me, his dull mind struggling for something scathing to say. But the half-wit thought better about crossing words with me again. He turned back to his father.

"Stay in the light!" he snapped and lumbered away.

I joined Spiros under the streetlight. The old man's face reflected his misery and shame.

"Why do you hang around?" he said. "Maybe you come here just so you can laugh at me?"

"I don't come to laugh!" I protested. "You are my friend, and I enjoy spending time with you."

"Go away and leave me in peace," he said.

I thought it best to allow him to calm down and started to walk away.

"Nikos," he called after me.

I turned back and saw his slight, forlorn figure beside his wagon.

"I'm sorry," he said remorsefully. "I didn't mean it when I said you should go away."

I hastened to reassure him.

"I'll return tomorrow, old friend," I said, "if only to taste more of your matchless hot dogs. My stomach cannot survive without them."

"Business was slow this afternoon," he said. "You only had two."

"I was hoping for at least four." I paused. "Tell me, Spiros, all day you sell hot dogs and pass the rejects to me. Yet I've never seen you eat one yourself."

He peered around carefully to make sure we were alone.

"They are an abomination," he said in a low, shaken voice. "I ate one years ago and nearly died."

"I'll keep those happy tidings between us," I said as I waved good-bye.

"Come back soon, Nikos," his voice carried plaintively across the gathering twilight. "Please, come back soon . . ."

As luck would have it, the cretin dishwasher who came on nights went on an extended drunk, and I had to work an additional six hours every day. I finished work at ten, several hours after Spiros wheeled his wagon away, so I didn't see him for a week.

The first evening the dishwasher returned, I wouldn't speak to the sot but hurried down to the Harrison Street corner.

Spiros and his wagon weren't there. I walked around the block, thinking he might have changed his location, but didn't see him. Finally, I entered the Plaka lunchroom where a skinny waitress leaned on the counter chewing gum.

"Isn't Spiros out with the wagon today?" I asked.

She shook her head. "Didn't you hear? The old man had a heart attack and died a week ago."

I stared at her in shock while she continued chewing her gum. While I was immersed in dirty dishes, my friend had died.

"They had his funeral a few days ago in the Greek church over on LaSalle."

"Where did they bury him?"

"In the Greek cemetery on the South Side," she said.

I returned to the restaurant to pick up my ten-year-old Ford, a high-mileage clunker that I rarely drove. I was grateful when it started, and I drove south on Halsted to Eighty-seventh Street and then west toward the cemetery. On the way I thought of the years I had spent with the old man, listening to his stories. Lost as he was in the trappings of myth, I would miss him.

A clerk in the cemetery office told me the location of Spiros's grave in the Greek section. I bought a small bouquet of fresh flowers from the cemetery greenhouse and walked about a half mile through the monuments and markers to the old man's grave.

Some of the graves I passed were ragged and neglected, and others were neatly cared for with pale asters, purple daisies, and scarlet and white geraniums. Violet swallows flew from tree to tree, their birdsongs sweeping across the stillness of the cemetery.

When I reached Spiros's grave, the descending sun had cast purple shadows over the grassy mounds and tinted the foliage of a large oak tree standing nearby. The rows of tombstones adorned with cherubs and crosses slipped slowly into twilight.

I placed the bouquet beside the withered petals scattered across the freshly turned earth. Abused by his worthless sons, his days spent selling the wretched hot dogs he couldn't eat, Spiros was probably better off in the ground where he would no longer have to suffer all the grievous indignities that human flesh is heir to.

Suddenly, I glimpsed a flash of movement beside a nearby tombstone. I thought at first it might be a squirrel or a rabbit. An instant later, a wind smelling of dead flowers and garden mold blew across my cheeks. In spite of the warm weather, a shiver chilled my body.

I realized suddenly that all around me the birds had fallen silent. Into that stillness, a strange rustling sound carried from within the foliage of the oak tree. The rustling grew shriller and louder, and then I heard the hoarse echo of a voice. For an instant, I feared I'd stumbled upon grave looters.

The wind carrying the moldy, decaying smells blew stronger, whistling across the graves. All around me the gravestones seemed to grow larger, looming like apparitions against the fading light.

Then I swear I saw them, a ghostly phalanx emerging from the shadows that mantled the graves, phantoms whose bodies glittered in the twilight. I heard a savage, berating voice that might have been Achilles and a mournful voice that could have been Hector pleading. Around these voices clattered the metallic jangle and din of armor and swords.

Although I had not run in twenty years, I turned then and fled. Rushing through the thickening darkness I could feel hordes of tiny, clammy insects pelting my cheeks. Once I stumbled, fell to one knee, heard the clamor of startled crickets, and scrambled frantically back up. When I reached my car, out of breath and shaken to the bone, I hurled myself into the front seat. Fumbling with chilled fingers, I snapped on the engine and drove from that cemetery as if the devil himself were in pursuit!

In the weeks that followed, I convinced myself that I had been mistaken. The falling twilight and the wind whistling among the graves coupled with my vivid memory of Spiros's stories had befuddled me. There was also my strongly held philosophy that there was no supernatural, no mystery beyond the life we live. What I thought I saw that night had to be an illusion.

But there were other nagging, restless nights when I lay awake recalling those moments among the gravestones. At those times, my thoughts and feelings accused one another, racing back and forth, up and down, inside and out, until my firm grasp on reality grew limp as a dead man's hand. Then, reason and logic abandoned me and with them carried away a lifetime of suspicion and doubt. Defying every rational bone in my body, I was compelled to accept that what I had seen and heard in that haunted twilight had really been there.

Yet, in the ashes and ruins of my philosophy lay a shard of comfort. If those ghosts of old warriors had been truly resurrected by Spiros's passion and his faith, then my old friend, who had existed in a world of myths and stories, had found companions and would not rest alone in the dark, cold grave of death.

When I was a boy growing up in my father's immigrant parish on the South Side of Chicago, following the tradition of families in Greece, it wasn't uncommon to have marriages arranged by parents, who found older, more affluent men for their daughters. Some of these marriages worked out very well, but others, of course, produced disharmony and unhappiness.

In these days of liberated ladies, such matchmaking is much less common but still exists. Young girls can be tempted by security and older men by the bounty of a young wife. I made Mathon Sarlas a wise enough older man to understand the dangers inherent in such a marriage so that he might make the right choice.

The Rousing of Mathon Sarlas

AT THE AGE OF FIFTY-FIVE, MATHON SARLAS HAD BEEN a widower for ten years. His wife's death from cancer in 1988 had left him with two children to raise, a task he believed that everyone in his Greek Orthodox parish of St. Katherine's would have conceded he had done exceedingly well. Both his son and daughter had obtained their bachelor's degrees, one from Northwestern University and the other from the University of Illinois at Circle Campus. Both of them had also married. Two years earlier, his son, Peter, had wed a fine young girl of Greek descent. Afterward, they had moved to his wife's hometown of Worcester, Massachusetts, where Peter had joined her father's real estate firm. Less than a year after his son's marriage, his daughter, Dena, had married an engineer who worked for the Boeing Company in Seattle. Soon after their wedding, they also moved from Chicago to live in that West Coast city.

With both of his offspring having departed from Chicago, Mathon was left alone in the big nine-room house in West Rogers Park except for an acerbic-tongued old housekeeper, Kyra, who had joined their household soon after his marriage. Her long tenure of service, which included looking after the children following his wife's death, had gained the old woman a license of impertinence that she exercised freely.

When Mathon's daughter still lived at home, he had never been lonely. At dinner each evening, Dena, with her gift for making ordinary experiences dramatic, would tell him of events that had transpired during her day. Mathon had taken a vicarious pleasure in her delight. She also had many friends she had invited in for parties, and every weekend their house had been filled with the banter and laughter of young men and women.

Now, without any reason to go home in the evening, Mathon began staying longer in the office of his wholesale grocery. Sometimes he drove to eat dinner alone at one of the Halsted Street restaurants and arrive home in time to watch the ten o'clock news. But the programs were saturated with details of the foibles of their randy president and his affair with the doe-eyed intern. Mathon had voted for William Clinton and considered him a good president, but he was disappointed at the man's rampant promiscuity, which allowed the shamelessly sanctimonious Republican managers to press for his impeachment.

When Mathon would finally go to bed, he had trouble sleeping. Thinking of his son and daughter living so far away brought back memories of his beloved wife, who had died so young.

One morning that spring, he rose with his limbs aching and his body unrested and vented his aggravation at Kyra for the breakfast she served him.

"These eggs are too hard!" he said to her sharply, gesturing at his plate. "After all these years, you should know I like my eggs soft!"

"That henfruit is cooked exactly the way you've eaten it for years," Kyra said.

"I want my bloody eggs the way I want them!"

"What a bilious crosspatch you've become!" the old lady snapped. "Nothing satisfies you anymore! Why don't you get your breakfast at one of those fast-food pest holes and give us both a rest!"

As she disappeared into the kitchen, he stamped into the hall and pulled on his hat and coat. "Battle-ax!" he mumbled wrathfully. "Dried-up old dragon! All these bloody years in my house like a boil on my neck!"

Mathon remained irritated all morning in his office, snarling at a salesman and scolding his bookkeeper. He argued with a customer over the phone and lost a sizable order for produce. He realized he was behaving like an idiot and took a brisk walk around the neighborhood to calm down. When he returned to his office, he found Father Nick Vrontes, his parish priest from St. Katherine's, waiting for him.

"I didn't know you were planning a visit, Father Nick," Mathon greeted him warmly. "If you'd let me know you were coming, I wouldn't have kept you waiting."

"I was visiting another parishioner in the neighborhood and thought I'd stop in."

"I'm always glad to see you, Father," Matron said, "even if your pockets are full of raffle tickets."

"Be of good heart, Mathon," Father Nick smiled. "I've come today only to inquire into the condition of your soul."

"Today my soul hangs like a stalk of rotting bananas around my throat," Mathon said morosely. "Sit down, Father, and rest your feet."

"What do you hear from Dena and Peter?" the priest asked.

"They're both fine," Mathon said. "Peter e-mails me every other day while Dena prefers to phone. As far as I can tell, she seems happy. Her husband is a good man, but I don't understand why he couldn't have found work closer to Chicago." He sighed. "Dena made the whole house light up with her laughter. Now that she's gone, the house is a mausoleum managed by a witch with the tongue of an adder."

"Is Kyra still nagging you?" Father Nick laughed.

"Has she ever stopped? I haven't been able to get the best of that woman as long as she's lived with us. She waits until my guard slips, and then she slams in one of those poison-tipped barbs."

They sat in silence for a moment. The priest shifted restlessly in his chair. "Mathon," he began slowly, "the truth is that I had a special reason for passing by your office today."

"How much do you want, Father Nick?"

"Will you stop your endless chatter about money!" the priest cried. "Hearing you would make one think I visit my parishioners as if they were banks from which I make repeated withdrawals. There are other concerns more important than money." He waved a stern finger at Mathon. "Now stop interrupting me, please, and allow me a chance to speak."

"I'll be silent as a tombstone," Mathon said.

"Good." The priest drew in a deep breath. "Now then, listen to me, Mathon. You are fifty-six years old . . ."

"Fifty-five. I won't be fifty-six until October."

"All right, fifty-five then. That is still a number well into middle age. Your business is firmly established, and you are one of the most respected individuals in our parish. You have also been a devoted father, and now your children are married and living their own lives. You have a right to look to your own future." He hesitated a moment and then plunged on. "I think it's time you married again."

Mathon stared at the priest in shock.

"I thought you had given up nagging me about that years ago," Mathon said. "When my children were young, you kept telling me I should marry because they needed a mother's care. Now that they're grown and gone, how can you suggest I bind myself to a wife?"

"You put off my entreaties in those years saying you didn't want your children looked after by a strange woman," the priest said. "Now that your children are married and have embarked on their own lives, am I to believe that you're prepared to spend the remainder of your days writing up orders for bananas and grapefruit and your nights in your nine-room mausoleum fighting with Kyra?"

"I've been a widower for ten years now," Mathon said. "If I'm not stiff yet, neither do my limbs have the juice they once had. When I am through with a day's work, I am tired. You'd have me marry and go home to fight with two nagging women instead of one?" He paused. "Besides, to be candid, Father Nick, I have fallen into the habit of abstinence, and a wife might not appreciate that discipline."

"I'm not thinking in terms of sex," the priest said sternly. "There are other things marriage can provide. Companionship, and devotion."

"If it pleases you, I will get a dog."

"Mathon, listen to me. I appeal to your good sense. It isn't natural to live alone for the rest of your life. I'm not suggesting you marry some young nymph who will want you to take her dancing every night but a mature woman who can provide you companionship for the coming years."

"Where will I find such a woman? I haven't time or inclination to begin a lengthy search and courtship."

"There are respectable families in our parish with attractive daughters of marriageable age," Father Nick said. "Discreet inquiries to the family could be made."

"Are you suggesting an arranged marriage?" Mathon said in disbelief. "Father Nick, this is almost the millennium! Haven't you heard of women's liberation? Young women read Gloria Steinem and Betty Friedan more often than the Bible. Dena made me read most of *The Feminine Mystique,* which I must admit was a grueling task. If those militant feminists catch wind of you speaking about arranged marriages, they'd picket the church."

"Of course marriages aren't arranged as frequently as they were at one time," Father Nick said, "but even today not every family has a daughter who is a feminist. Some still endorse the old-fashioned virtues of a good marriage to an honorable man and recognize they need assistance in that regard."

Mathon shook his head impatiently.

"I can't believe what you're telling me, Father Nick! The next thing you'll suggest is that I marry Kyra and make her an honest woman. She couldn't make me any more miserable as my wife than she makes me now."

The priest rose stiffly. "If you cannot be serious, Mathon," he said, "there is no use in us talking further."

Mathon gestured in apology at the priest.

"I'll be serious, Father Nick," he said quietly, "but you be serious, too. You are not only my parish priest but one of my dearest friends. You are now concerned because I am living alone, and you volunteer to find me a wife. Will you find one who will love me because I am as handsome as Paul Newman or one who will accept me because I can buy her a fur coat and take her to Europe for a vacation every year?"

"You are a distinguished looking man, Mathon," the priest insisted. "Many women would find you attractive and be proud to be your wife." He started for the door. "Just think about it," he said. "That's all I ask. We can speak about it again."

"Bring your raffle books next time, Father," Mathon said. "I prefer signing checks to discussing my entering the bondage of marriage."

The priest paused in the doorway. "Kyra is right," he said reprovingly. "You are becoming a dyspeptic old grouch. I will suggest that she light a bigger candle for you in church on Sundays."

"If my salvation depends upon the old virago's candles," Mathon said gruffly, "I may renounce my faith and become a heathen."

After the priest had gone, Mathon sat at his desk for a long time. Finally, he rose and walked to the washbasin in the corner. He studied his reflection in the mirror. His good head of hair, graying at the temples, did make him look distinguished. He also didn't believe his face reflected his age. Stepping away from the basin and looking down at his waist, he was distressed at the small bulge of flesh that pressed against his belt. When he inhaled and puffed out his chest, the bulge disappeared.

With a sudden start, he saw the face of his bookkeeper reflected in the mirror. He whirled around with a quick cough to cover his confusion.

"What do you want, Telis?" he cried. "Can't you knock? I have a headache and was looking for some aspirin."

"I'm sorry, Mathon," his bookkeeper said apologetically. "I knocked several times, but you didn't hear me. I have some prices for you on the Veremis order."

"I'll look at them later," Mathon said impatiently. "Go send out a few statements and see if you can collect some of our overdue accounts."

The bookkeeper hurried out of the office. Mathon walked back to his desk. He tried to concentrate on a sheaf of invoices.

"That priest must be mad to come pursuing me now after all these years," he muttered. "The whole idea is ridiculous!"

But in the days that followed, Mathon couldn't put the thought of a wife out of his mind. As spring came to the city around him, the seed planted by the priest was nourished in the winter of his loneliness. He found it more and more difficult to keep his thoughts involved on business. He also developed a greater measure of sympathy for his lascivious president.

During the years of their marriage, he and his wife had enjoyed a satisfactory sex life, probably more active than some and not as active as others. After her death, for a while his grief and distress had suppressed any thought of sex. When he started to feel sexual desire again and found himself plagued by vagrant longings, he had resorted to relieving himself as he had done when he was a youth.

The truth was that the hours he had spent looking after his business and the evenings and weekends caring for his young son and daughter had left him little time or energy for erotic fantasies. When he thought of men sentenced to long terms in prison or to other men dedicated to the celibate priesthood in the Roman Catholic Church, he came to believe that abstinence could become as natural a way of life as promiscuity. As for whatever pleasure sexual intimacy might have provided him, the welfare of his son and daughter had been ample compensation for that loss.

A week after the visit of the priest to his office, he began to diet, and a few days later, while doing some business downtown, on an impulse he walked into Marshall Field's and had himself measured for a new suit.

"You're a fool, Mathon," he said as he glared at his reflection in the full-length dressing room mirror. "Do you think the pigeons will come flying into your arms just because you wrap your middle-aged bones in a new suit?"

But as the erotic thoughts persisted, a new fear rose to plague him. After all his years of abstinence, might his genitals have atrophied? He was reassured the following morning when he woke with a rampant erection.

In his new condition of awakened sexuality, he discovered the plethora of sex sites on the Internet. In the evening after his employees had gone home, he nervously surfed the Web on the computer in his office. He was shocked at the sexual aberrations the Internet provided in vivid and colorful abundance.

Suddenly, the barriers and restraints he had fashioned over the years began to crumble. He was distressed at his wanton thoughts. For the first time, he began to regard several younger women in his office as more than employees. He found various excuses for one of them, Milly Bakunis, who had a full, lovely figure—and who was already married—to come into his office. Once, as she bent close to where he sat at his desk to show him some orders, he inhaled the fragrance of her perfume and found himself trembling.

He began furtively appraising women he passed on the street. Too young, he would think about one, much too young. She looks as if she's a sophomore in college. Too frozen, he would think of another; a laugh might crack her cheeks. When he saw a woman that appealed to him, he considered boldly what she would be like as his wife, sharing his table and his bed.

One Sunday morning in late April, about a month after Father Nick had spoken to him about marriage, Cleon Argiris, one of the church trustees, came to the pew where Mathon sat and whispered that Father Nick wished to see him after church. After the liturgy, Mathon lingered in the narthex amid the cloying scents of candles until the priest came walking down the center aisle with his black cassock swirling about his ankles.

"I'm sorry to have delayed you, Mathon," Father Nick said crisply, "but I wonder if you'd be kind enough to drop off some material for our commemorative album at Perry Cosmos's print shop? It's right on your way."

"Gladly, Father."

"Come into my office," the priest said. "I have the material there."

Mathon followed Father Nick into the church office and found it occupied by several people. There was an older man, his face wizened as a dried fig, and a stout woman with a large flowered hat. There was also a girl he took to be their daughter.

"If you're busy, Father Nick, I'll wait outside until you've finished."

"That's all right, Mathon," Father Nick said. "I'm having lunch with the Gatsis family. George, may I present Mr. Mathon Sarlas."

Mr. Gatsis rose quickly. "Mr. Sarlas is known to everyone in the parish for his civic generosity," he said with pronounced respect. He extended his lean, bony hand. "It is an honor, Mr. Sarlas." He motioned to the woman and the girl. "May I present my wife, Sophia, and our daughter, Nikki?"

"A pleasure," Mathon said politely, and for a moment his gaze met the girl's eyes. She appeared perhaps in her late twenties or even early thirties, an attractive girl with black hair and fine skin and a mouth that seemed just a little wide for her slender face. Her hand in Mathon's clasp was slim-fingered and soft to his touch.

"I worked on a committee once with Mr. Sarlas, who was chairman." Sophia Gatsis's teeth glittered as she smiled. She emitted a coy little laugh. "Of course he wouldn't remember me."

"I do remember you," Mathon said. "That was the committee for the Pan Arcadian Convention last year."

Mrs. Gatsis gave a small cry of pleasure and looked triumphantly at her husband.

"Mathon has an excellent memory," Father Nick said. He handed Mathon a small wrapped package. "Thank you again, Mathon, for dropping it off."

"Good-bye, Mr. Sarlas." Mr. Gatsis extended his bony hand once more.

"Good-bye," Mathon said. He smiled at Sophia and at Nikki. The girl murmured a polite farewell.

Mathon left the church office and did not realize until he was outside on the street that he had been holding himself stiff and erect to create an impression of having a trimmer figure. He grimaced at his vanity and at the obvious duplicity of the priest in arranging the meeting. At the same time, he marveled at how attractive the girl was. He couldn't imagine that she wouldn't have a number of young men vying for her affection.

That evening, he waited for the call from the priest. When the phone rang, he called to Kyra that he would answer and then carried the portable phone into the bedroom, away from the old lady's sharp ears.

"Mathon?" Father Nick's voice hummed across the wire.

"Hello, Father," Mathon said amiably. "I delivered the package to the printer. How was your lunch with the Gatsis family?"

"Fine," Father Nick said. "They are a wonderful family." He paused. "Mathon?"

"Yes, Father?"

"What did you think of Nikki Gatsis?"

"She's a very attractive young woman."

"You think so?" The priest spoke with evident satisfaction. "What did you think of her parents?"

"Why?" Mathon asked smugly. "Do I have to marry all three of them?"

There was a moment of silence.

"I'm afraid my matchmaking skills have grown rusty," the priest murmured. "Was it as obvious as all that?"

"Yes, Father," Mathon said. "But more important than my reaction, what did the girl think of me?"

"It is too soon to know for sure," Father Nick said. "But when I spoke to George Gatsis alone, he told me she was impressed with you, that she spoke of you with respect."

"I expect respect from my bookkeeper," Mathon said. "I want love and companionship."

"Mathon, are you well?" the priest asked. "The last time I mentioned this matter, you were outraged. What has changed your mind?"

"I've just been thinking about the prospect of marriage, Father Nick. I still have some reservations, but I am ready to be convinced."

"Splendid!" the priest said with excitement in his voice. "This girl is very bright, a little shy perhaps, but these days that's a rare and commendable trait. She has also attended business college for two years."

"You know I only finished high school. Maybe she won't find me well enough educated."

"Mathon, be serious now. I have known this family for many years. George Gatsis operates a small notions and souvenir shop, and the family is very respectable and devout. Sophia Gatsis has had some medical problems, and I think they are under financial pressure. Nikki has been working for the last few years as a secretary and still lives at home." The priest paused. "In two months she will be thirty. Her parents feel it is time for her to be married to a member of our parish, perhaps a man a little older who has never been married or to a widower. When I suggested that perhaps you might be interested, both her father and mother were delighted. And the girl, Nikki, now that she has seen you, does not seem displeased."

"All right, Father," Mathon said. "Since you are more versed than I am in the rituals of matchmaking, what do we do next?"

"Sophia will phone to invite you over one evening for dinner," Father Nick said. "If that goes well, a few nights later you might invite Nikki out to dinner and perhaps the theater. Give yourselves

an opportunity to get to know each other. Then, if you both remain interested and wish to proceed, we can discuss the matter
further."

"I'll be expecting their call," Mathon said.

"Mathon?"

"Yes, Father?"

"I must say I find this reversal of your attitude toward marriage
most gratifying."

"Ever since you spoke to me, Father Nick," Mathon said, "I find
myself leering at every woman I pass on the street. That is also true
of the married women employed in my office. I am concerned that
I will lose control and assault one of them."

"Shame on you, Mathon!" the priest cried. "You're a wicked man
who enjoys tormenting me! I don't know why I bother with you!"

Mathon began the whole business half as a lark, not really believing the girl could be interested in him. He also felt a certain
uneasiness because Nikki wasn't that many years older than his
own daughter.

But when Sophia Gatsis phoned to invite him for dinner, he
accepted, and on that Friday evening he went to their apartment
carrying flowers for Nikki, a box of Godiva chocolates for her
mother, and a bottle of fine brandy for her father.

The evening went off much better than he had anticipated. Sophia Gatsis was a splendid cook, and the dinner she prepared was
delicious. George Gatsis had a wry sense of humor and told some
good stories. As for Nikki, although she did not say a great deal,
she seemed to respond favorably to what he was saying. At the end
of the evening, full of wine and good food, Mathon left the Gatsis
house thinking that something fortuitous might develop from the
whole business, after all.

A few days later, he phoned to invite Nikki to dinner. He was
pleased when she accepted, and on the following Saturday evening he took her to dinner at one of the more elegant downtown
restaurants.

Away from the inhibiting influence of her parents, Nikki smiled
more often and spoke more freely. He found that looking at her
and listening to her afforded him pleasure. He sought to make

her understand that he didn't regard himself as some impetuous and dashing suitor but a mature family man seeking affection and companionship.

That evening was followed by several more. He was encouraged to phone her again because she seemed to genuinely enjoy their evenings together. She began speaking to him more candidly of her life at home and about her job, which she disliked. She would have preferred to remain in school but had to begin working to help her parents. She also confided in him—a little bitterly, he thought—about a young man she had cared for who had found another girl and broken off their relationship.

"My father and mother were happy about his leaving, of course," Nikki said pensively, "but I was hurt. For a long while there were nights when I cried myself to sleep."

Her confession filled Mathon with compassion, and in response he found himself pouring out his own heart, telling her of the lonely years following his wife's death when he had raised their children. He also spoke of his desire to find someone with whom to share his life. For the first time that evening he saw tears glistening in Nikki's eyes. She reached out and gently, consolingly, touched his hand.

One of the things that bothered him was the obvious eagerness of her parents for their union. They fawned over him whenever he visited their apartment. At those moments Nikki appeared resentful, an unhappy girl caught in the web of some filial obligation. Mathon tried earnestly to make them all understand that he was the one who felt grateful and honored.

During those weeks that Nikki and he went out together, their only intimacy was holding hands. He felt that as long as he remained uncommitted, he could still draw back before making himself appear too great a fool. But he felt a stirring of desire in his flesh and found himself yearning to hold her. He even allowed himself to fantasize what making love to her would be like.

There was a night near the end of May when Nikki and he shared an early dinner. As they were driving home from the restaurant, she nestled her head gently against his shoulder, an intimacy he found immensely pleasurable. The beam of street lamps they passed swept her cheeks and eyes in and out of shadow. He was possessed by a sudden shaken tenderness, and as they pulled up before her house, it suddenly seemed quite natural for him to gently kiss her lips. He wasn't prepared for her swift recoiling from him, as if he had burned her mouth by his touch.

She sought quickly to make amends, laughing nervously, telling him that she had been half-asleep and he had startled her. She held his hand tightly and kissed him, a quick, faint brushing of her lips across his mouth.

He walked Nikki to the front door of the apartment building, and she asked him to come upstairs. He told her he was tired and would go on home. After she had entered the building he sat for a while in his car. He recalled his feelings as a young man when he had courted his wife and the excitement and anticipation he had felt when she accepted his proposal of marriage. He recalled their delight at the birth of their children and the many happy days and nights they had shared as a family.

He left the car, walked into the apartment hallway, and rang the Gatsis bell. When the buzzer sounded, he ascended the stairs to their apartment.

Nikki answered the door, and he smiled to reassure her and asked to speak to her father and mother. In a few moments they all gathered in the parlor, her father in shirt, trousers, and slippers, the newspaper he'd been reading still clutched in his hand. Sophia Gatsis came from the kitchen with flour stains across the bosom of her apron.

"Forgive me for intruding at this hour," he spoke quietly to the three of them, "but there is something I wish to say and think it better not to wait any longer." He turned to Nikki, whose large, dark eyes watched him uneasily. "Nikki," he said gently, "we have been going out together for several weeks now, and you must know that you have become precious to me. You must know that I have been considering asking you to be my wife." He felt a tightness in his chest and drew a deep breath. "Now, I am nearly twice your age. I have a son and daughter only a few years younger than you are. You have become very dear to me, but I don't want you to make a mistake."

"She will not make a mistake, Mr. Sarlas," Sophia Gatsis said shrilly.

"She is genuinely fond of you, Mathon," George Gatsis said anxiously.

"Please, let Nikki speak for herself," Mathon said quietly. He looked back at the girl, who stood stiffly watching him.

"If you consented to marry me," he said, "I would promise to love you and care for you. You'd be able to do whatever you wished to do, and we could also travel and see the world." He paused, a pensiveness entering his voice. "The only thing I wouldn't be able to give you is youth to match your own. In ten or fifteen years, when I am a much older man, you would still be a fairly young woman. Do you understand?"

"She understands," Sophia Gatsis said quickly. "Mr. Sarlas, I am sure she understands."

"Do you understand?" Mathon repeated earnestly.

"Yes," she said, and a trace of resentfulness entered her voice. "You don't have to talk to me like Mama and Papa do. I'm not a blind little fool. I understand."

"Do you?" he pressed her. "Are you sure?"

"I said I understood!" she could not meet his eyes and looked sullenly away. "I don't care about your age."

"She is a sensible girl," George Gatsis said. "She wants mature love." He appealed desperately to his wife. "Isn't that the kind of girl she is?"

"Forgive me, but I don't think you're telling me the truth," Mathon said to Nikki. "I think you are trying to please your parents and trying to convince yourself that financial security would make everything all right. But this evening, when I kissed you, for the first time you understood what marriage to me would really mean for you."

"Mathon," George Gatsis pleaded, "this kind of talk is not proper. Let Nikki give you her decision tomorrow."

"I feel we must talk now," Mathon said. He turned again to the girl. "Nikki," he said, "do you think you could ever love me?"

"Mr. Sarlas!" Sophia Gatsis cried.

There was a long, tense silence in the room. George Gatsis crumpled a corner of the newspaper in his hand. Sophia Gatsis breathed in short, harsh gasps. "Nikki . . ." she said, making a gesture of entreaty toward her daughter.

"I don't know," Nikki spoke in a thin, toneless whisper.

"I know," Mathon said, and a great weariness and resignation swept his flesh. "I know that if you married me, you'd be terribly unhappy, more unhappy than you are now. You would resent me and might even come to hate me. And that would hurt me more than any loneliness I feel now."

Suddenly, Nikki began to cry. Her lips trembled and the tears came slowly and sorrowfully from her eyes, staining her cheeks. "I'm sorry," she said. "I'm so sorry."

"I am sorry, too," Mathon said quietly. "But not as sorry as we would both be if we made this mistake. He turned and spoke to Sophia and George Gatsis. "Don't blame Nikki," he said. "I am the one to blame by letting myself believe that I might live my life and my first love over again."

The following Sunday evening, Father Nick came to dinner at Mathon's home. They sat at the table in the dining room while Kyra served them roast chicken and rice. They spoke of church matters and carefully avoided the subject on both their minds. When their wine glasses were empty, Mathon filled them again from the decanter.

"Enough, enough," the priest said with a sigh. "If I drink anymore, I may not find my way home." He looked earnestly at Mathon. "I suppose, my friend," he said, "after this debacle I had best never speak to you of marriage again."

"By this one effort, Father Nick," Mathon smiled, "you have more than fulfilled your responsibility to me."

"We might seek an older, more mature woman," Father Nick said cautiously. "I think my misjudgment here was that Nikki Gatsis was simply too young."

"I am not sure I want an older, more mature woman," Mathon shrugged. "A woman set in her ways the way I am set in mine. Frankly, Father Nick, I see no urgency for me to look for anyone to marry. What I prefer to do is explore the various avenues for erotic pleasure that exist in this permissive society. I am a single male and I have money and I should be able to have a good time."

"Mathon!" the priest said sternly. "Are you suggesting you will now indulge in a licentious and promiscuous life?"

"I think so, Father," Mathon said amiably. "Let's say I plan to test the waters. I don't expect to rival the playboy Hugh Hefner, but I should be able to find a few attractive women who would like to share a good time. If I find someone who seems special and who is also attracted to me, why, I might then consider marriage. But not yet . . . I'm not in any hurry."

"Mathon, don't do anything rash, now!" Father Nick pleaded. "You're a mature and respectable man and should not begin a routine of dalliance. Think of what people in the parish would say."

"Frankly, good Father Nick, I don't much care what people in the parish will say. I have buried my beloved wife and raised my children. For whatever years I still have ahead of me, I will now seek and take my pleasure where I find it."

The priest stared at him in dismay.

"Mathon!" he said hoarsely. "I've done this to you! I couldn't leave you alone and let things as they were. I had to bring the demon of sexuality into your life! How will I ever forgive myself?"

Kyra had entered the dining room. She moved stiffly around the table and picked up a few plates. Mathon looked at her and felt a flash of inspiration.

"Father Nick, it isn't you who has awakened my sexuality," Mathon said. "What has set me on fire is having to live daily around Kyra. I begin to see beneath her sullen exterior what a stunningly passionate woman she really is! I shake with desire at the sight of her!"

Kyra let loose a squawk of indignation.

"Do you hear him, Father!" the old woman shrilled and slammed her bony fist against the table. "Do you hear the shameless lecher? I don't know what's gotten into the old goat, but I'm a decent woman and won't tolerate such talk!"

"Mathon," the priest tried to restrain a smile. "Stop it now."

"I can't help myself, Father! She drives me mad with desire!"

The old woman let loose a shriek of outrage and fled furiously to the kitchen. She stuck her head back in the door.

"You dirty old goat!" she cried balefully. "Wait until I write the children!"

"Tell them I am batty about you!" Mathon shouted. When she slammed the kitchen door, he winked at the priest. "For the first time in twenty years," he whispered in delight, "I have the old dragon on the run."

"Shame on you, Mathon," Father Nick said. "Is that something to be proud of?"

"Indeed it is, Father!" Mathon chortled and shook his head. "Indeed it is."

Legends of Glory

Our eldest son, Mark, and our youngest son, Dean, live in California with their families, which include three of our grandchildren, Alexis, Nicholas, and Adriana. A third son, John, lives in Chicago with his wife, Lynn, and their ten-year-old son—our fourth grandchild—Lucas, a bright and handsome child (as all children are to their grandparents). Because they reside not far from our home in northwest Indiana, they are the part of the family we see most often. For years now, every ritual we share—birthdays, holidays, the beginning of each new school year—creates its own joy and music. I am also witness to how integral a part Lucas is in his parents' lives, their pride and delight in him requiring a poet's eloquence.

From that awareness, it requires only a small leap to imagine Lucas growing into manhood, going to war, and, the nightmare of every family with a son or daughter in the military, being killed in battle. How would we as a family bear such a loss? Yet our love for Lucas is no greater than the love other parents and grandparents feel, our sorrow if we lost him no greater than the sorrow other parents and grandparents would experience with the death of a son or a daughter.

I began this novella to vent my feelings of despair and frustration about the human cost of the war in Iraq, both the wounding and deaths of our own soldiers and the wounding and deaths of tens of thousands of Iraqi civilians. By the time I had finished, however, the story no longer concerned the politics of a war that has bitterly divided our nation but became an effort to convey the enormity of a loss that tears asunder the natural cycle of the generations whereby sons and daughters bury their parents. I wanted to write not only of the untimely death of the young but of how parents and grandparents struggle to accommodate to life after such a death. I suspect there are families who never find peace but remain figures in mourning for as long as they live.

Chapter 1

DAN SCOTT COULDN'T REMEMBER A WINTER AS LONG and punishing. The small Indiana town of Provincefield where he lived, across the lake from Chicago, lay in the South Bend–to–Michigan City snowbelt. Half a dozen blizzards had struck the region during January and February. These lumbering snowfalls were followed in March and April by bitter cold that had prevented the mounds of snow from melting. In early May, a few perennials had budded fleetingly in search of spring, then withered in the frozen nights.

The desolate, endless season seemed to reflect the country in the winter of its discontent. In addition to the ongoing problems of crime, drug traffic, corruption, and general indifference toward the plight of the poor and the aged, the country was mired in a savage and fallacious war, started for one reason that proved baseless and now being fought for another untenable premise, the democratization of a nation torn by tribal and religious rivalries. The Iraqi conflict that had begun in March of 2003 with a swift victory (a bombing of Baghdad so lethal it had been designated "Shock and Awe") had deteriorated into a nightmare of booby-trapped cars and suicide bombings.

Sending a son or daughter to war had to be hard enough for parents who believed the conflict was justified. But it was even more ravaging for parents such as Dan and Molly who thought the war a calamitous blunder.

Yet, despite their own feelings, their son, Noah, had made the decision to enlist in the U.S. Marine Corps in the summer of 2004. After completing boot camp, called the "Crucible" for the harsh severity of its training, he was sent overseas in September. They received one letter from him while he was based in Kuwait, and the letters that followed came from Baghdad, where his unit had been deployed. May would mark Noah's eighth month in that bereaved country.

Dan drove into the lot adjoining Provincefield High School where he taught honors English and literature classes to juniors and seniors and parked in his usual spot under a small grove of trees adjoining the football field. During the winter, the skeletal branches had been silhouetted against a bleak landscape. That morning, he noticed for the first time pale, fragile buds on the branches, an augury of renewal that induced a flutter of hope in his heart. Perhaps, during the summer or by autumn, conditions in Iraq might improve and U.S. troops could begin to withdraw. But as quickly as that fantasy took shape, reality throttled it once more. The chaos in that battle-torn land wasn't improving but growing worse for its own citizens as well as for the occupying forces. For every American soldier who died in battle, a hundred

Iraqi men, women, and children perished in the carnage. While Dan felt compassion for their plight, his greatest fear was for his own son.

There were nights he lay awake in bed beside Molly, feeling his breathing shallow and labored, his chest and shoulders cramped. After visiting the doctor, where his fear of heart problems proved unfounded, he came to understand it was stress that constricted his breath and tensed his muscles. Hearing his wife stirring fitfully beside him, he knew she was tense and sleepless as well, her fear greater than his own. She was Noah's mother, and he was their only child.

Despite his anxiety, Dan tried to appear positive in the school and the town. Provincefield's residents had adopted Noah as their son, taking pride in one of their own joining a corps whose motto was "First to fight for right and freedom and to keep our honor clean." A number of his neighbors as well as townspeople he did not know tied yellow ribbons to the trees before their houses to honor his son's service. For weeks after Noah's departure, the VFW Post in Provincefield displayed the words "GOD SPEED, NOAH" on the billboard outside their headquarters building.

If Dan still lived in the more populous city of Hammond, Indiana, where he'd been born and gone to school, his turmoil might pass unnoticed. But in their small town, he was asked constantly about Noah. As the father of a marine serving in Iraq, Dan could not shame his son by revealing his own fears to others.

However well-intentioned people were, Dan found the endless queries wearying. In the span of an afternoon, he uttered the same meaningless phrases of reassurance to Connie Wertham in the post office, Avery Dolton at the bank, and Jeff Clements, the pharmacist at CVS. Their town librarian, Emily Fletcher, meeting him on the street, asked him to stop by the library to pick up material she had researched on the history of the Marine Corps, which had been founded when the first two battalions had been authorized by the Continental Congress in 1775. Meanwhile, students at the high school pointed him out as "the father of the Prov' High graduate and football star fighting in Iraq."

Even in the seclusion of his own home, he could not escape being reminded of his son. Pastor Robert Wiggam of St. James

Presbyterian Church, where Dan and Molly attended, had phoned him excitedly the evening before to tell him he'd received a letter from Noah. Norm Beavers, owner of the Ace Hardware store and a former marine, dropped by the house to chat and explain to Dan how the "bloodstripe," the red stripe down the leg of the blue marine uniform, represented the blood that had been shed in battle by marines for more than 200 years.

Once, listening to Ted Koppel on *Nightline* reading the names of the young men and young women soldiers killed in Iraq, Dan thought he'd heard his son's name.

In the months Noah had been away, Dan—waiting tensely for each day's news from Iraq—was assailed by memories from the past. They came to him as he watched a group of children in a playground or saw a child holding his mother's hand in the supermarket. But they also came abruptly at unrelated moments: listening to a student reciting in the classroom, drinking a cup of coffee in the teacher's lounge, filling his car with gas in a town station.

He recalled the joy and gratefulness he and Molly felt when, following Molly's two miscarriages, Noah was born. The miracle occurred after they had despaired of ever having a child.

The small, cherished baby they first brought home grew bigger and stronger with each passing month, tottering on unsteady legs as he walked for the first time. There was kindergarten, and a year later, first grade. Dan would never forget the poignant sight of the child he left at the door of the first-grade classroom, small bag of lunch clutched desperately in his hand, casting a beseeching look at his father as Dan waved him good-bye.

After their childless years, Noah brought a new wonder and delight into their lives. As he neared the end of his long day of teaching, Dan would anticipate arriving home. When he entered the house, Noah would shout and run to greet him, hugging his knees tightly, making Dan feel needed and loved.

Another recurring image was one of lying beside his son in bed at night while he read Noah stories: Dr. Seuss, *The Little Engine That Could*, a children's book on King Arthur and the Knights of the Round Table, and later, when Noah was older, the *Iliad* of Homer. As he read, Dan would steal glimpses at his son's enraptured eyes. After Noah had fallen asleep, Dan often remained beside the bed, staring down at his son's face in the soft glow of the nightlight. In those moments, he felt a surge of pity for parents who were childless.

During the December holidays, they'd drive to the Christmas tree farm across the state line in Michigan. Clad in thick fleece jacket and boots, Noah would lurch and stumble from tree to tree in the ridges of snow until he found the one he was seeking and cried, "This one, Papa! This is the one!" They'd cut the tree down, tie it to the top of the car, and haul it home. Dan would string the lights while Noah handed him the ornaments, telling him, as if every ornament had a special significance, where to hang them on the tree.

On Christmas Eve, Molly would pin Noah's stocking over the fireplace. They'd go through the ritual of placing a plate of cookies and a small glass of milk on a table nearby, nourishment for Santa on his wearying journey in and out of houses.

Noah would wake them Christmas morning by leaping into their bed. He'd lead them excitedly downstairs, and they would open the presents from family and friends. And, finally, when the time came to put childhood fantasies away, Noah accepted without dismay that he had outgrown the myth, referring to it gravely as "that stuff they tell kids."

As Noah grew older, graduating from elementary school and entering high school, he became a companion with whom Dan shared adventures. They'd take excursions for the day into Chicago to visit the Museum of Science and Industry, Shedd Aquarium, and Adler Planetarium.

Noah had shown a special interest in astronomy, and Dan and Molly bought him a telescope for his fourteenth birthday. For weeks afterward, on cloudless nights, they'd spend hours peering at the sky, tracking Saturn, Mercury, and Venus and the constellations of Andromeda and Orion.

They'd also travel into Chicago to watch Cubs or White Sox games. When Noah began playing high school baseball, he displayed for the first time his talent for athletics. Perhaps nurtured by some gene in their ancestry that had skipped over Dan, who had been only an average player, Noah had the instinct and timing of a natural athlete. That early promise was fulfilled when Noah won track meets as a freshman in Provincefield High and, in the following few years, excelled in both baseball and football. When he concentrated his efforts on football, he became one of the best running backs in the state of Indiana, twice helping take his team to state finals and once, competing against thirty teams from a half dozen states, winning a Midwestern Regional trophy. After a triumphant game against some rival school, it wasn't uncommon to find an action photograph of Noah in their local paper, the *Provincefield Gazette.*

Noah hadn't been only a fine athlete but also an excellent student who consistently received high grades. In addition to his athletic and scholastic achievements, his grace of bearing and congenial disposition made him popular among his teachers as well as his fellow students. The entry under his smiling photo in the senior yearbook read, "Tom Cruise, beware!"

As much as the war and Noah's safety haunted Dan, he knew his wife's ordeal was even harder. Her anguish was fueled by a terror she had lived with through the years when Noah was growing into manhood. Molly was bitterly convinced that their son's military service had been decided for him generations before he was born.

The Scotts were a military family. Although Dan had grown up between the country's wars and never felt any compulsion to enlist in the armed services, Scotts had fought and died in every war since the Civil War. Dan's father, Thomas Joshua Scott, eighty-eight years old, lived with them from the time Noah was twelve until he turned sixteen, at which time his father moved to the Veterans' Home in Cranston. Thomas Scott had fought in World War II, earning a Medal of Honor for exceptional valor during the landings on D-Day at Omaha Beach. In later battles, he had been given the nickname "Tracker" for his ability to search out and kill snipers.

Thomas Scott vowed there had been Scotts in the Revolutionary War, even though their service hadn't been recorded. What could be confirmed was that four Scott brothers had been soldiers in the Civil War, all serving in the Union Army of the Tennessee under the command of Major General Ulysses S. Grant. One died at Shiloh, and another lost his life at Chickamauga. One of the two Scotts who survived was Dan's great-grandfather, who had two sons and two daughters. His great-grandfather's brother, Edmund, the other Civil War survivor, had three sons. Each of these forebears contributed one son to the Spanish-American War, and Edmund's son had been killed in the charge up San Juan Hill with Teddy Roosevelt.

Dan's grandfather had been one of three Scotts who served in World War I, one of them dying in the Second Battle of the Marne in July 1918. His own father and his uncle Charley fought in World War II; his uncle was killed in the Battle of the Bulge. Dan had five cousins who fought in either Korea or Vietnam, one of them dying in each of those conflicts.

The First Gulf War, launched when Saddam Hussein, the dictator of Iraq, invaded Kuwait in 1990, had ended so quickly that Dan's two Scott cousins of military age had little chance to enlist. Now, twelve years later, with the outbreak of the second Iraq war, the only Scott men besides Noah were near Dan's own age of fifty. If Noah hadn't enlisted, it would have been the first American war in at least 150 years where a Scott hadn't taken part.

Molly's belief that their son had been trapped in the military history of their family was reinforced by the imposing presence and force of Dan's father. When Dan's mother, Jennifer, died in 1992, his father had been retired for almost ten years from his job as a Rolling Mill foreman at the U.S. Steel Works in Gary. When his health declined, hip and leg problems impeding his ability to walk, Thomas Scott sold his house in Hammond in 1996 and, at the urging of Dan and Molly, moved to Provincefield to live with them.

As a boy growing up in Hammond, Dan had heard his father's stories of the Omaha Beach landing that included thousands of landing craft and 500 naval vessels that had sailed from British ports to invade the French coast. From his father's vivid recitals, he could almost envision the battle in which two American divisions had landed on Omaha Beach and Utah Beach while two British divisions and one Canadian division had landed on Gold Beach, Juno Beach, and Sword Beach. Dan could still see his father's rugged, expressive face and hear his strong voice, honed and bulwarked through years of working in the clangorous mills, reconstructing the events of that day.

"A British sailor on our landing craft told us, 'Mates, when we drop this ramp you better get off quick because we're pushing right back out to sea!' But before we could hit the beach, our craft struck some steel pilings the Germans had sunk in the water. But the Brits lowered the ramp anyway and Lieutenant Cardoza was the first man off, thrashing through the sea that was almost up to his throat, waving at us to follow him. By God, we couldn't let the man go in alone, and as we scrambled off into the water, firing from the shore came at us in a tremendous volley, some small-arms fire but also machine guns peppering the water all around us. There was about a hundred yards of open beach in front of us and, along the beach, homes like those you see here along the lake. We didn't know if the firing was coming from them.

"By then mortars and 88s were landing around us, sending up explosions of water and sand. I saw one of our guys, Norm Rankin, holding his rifle in the air in one hand and his rosary in the other, and then he was hit and went under. I saw other guys caught in the rough water who, scared of drowning, tossed away their rifles and even tore off parts of their uniforms so when we got to the beach, men came crawling out of the water nearly naked, not looking like tough, battle-ready soldiers but like boys out for a swim who got caught in a typhoon.

"Everywhere I looked there were chunks of wreckage, floating arms and legs, bodies of drowned men washing in across the beach. Through the noise and smoke, I could see Lieutenant Cardoza still standing, still waving us forward, and those of us who had survived the bullets and the water ran toward him. We fell on our bellies, crawling under the barbed wire, and I could hear those machine guns whistling rounds over our heads. I saw men not far from me touch off land mines and get blown to hell."

On and on the stories went, through Dan's childhood and into his adolescence. Then he heard his father repeating them to Noah and to friends who came to their house to visit.

Dan was grateful for his father's survival and proud of his achievements but had little interest in the stories of war. However, those weren't the feelings of Noah. As a child visiting his grandparents' house in Hammond and then in the hours he spent with his grand-father after Thomas Scott moved into their home in Provincefield, Noah listened eagerly to the stories of war. From his childhood into his adolescence, the boy sat enthralled at his grandfather's knees, his face glowing with the excitement of the narrative. Noah came to know the stories of battle and heroism so well that if his grandfather altered a sentence or an episode, Noah excitedly corrected him. Dan had the feeling that his father deliberately recast the narrative for the pleasure of hearing his grandson earnestly correcting his version.

"By God, boy, you're right!" Thomas Scott would cry, slapping his knee with his broad, strong hand. "I'd forgotten that part of the story!"

It wasn't only his own war experiences that his father recounted to Noah. Thomas Scott told equally vivid stories about the battles in which earlier generations of Scotts had fought, from Shiloh and Chickamauga through World War I and into Korea and Vietnam. The old soldier knew every detail of each battle, beginning with the Civil War and the exploits of Captain Abner Scott, who had commanded Company D of the 51st Indiana Infantry and who received the first Scott family Medal of Honor for leading his regi-ment over five lines of the rebel entrenchments at Shiloh before he fell, fatally wounded.

Moving forward through each of the nation's wars that followed the Civil War, his father zealously narrated the actions of every Scott, including their individual acts of heroism and the decora-tions they had earned despite fire and fear, doing "the honorable thing." In his father's stories, a nation's warriors were the noblest manifestation of its spirit, the quintessence of its highest ideals. In his assessment of history and his judgment of nations, there could be no more exemplary mission than fidelity to one's country in a time of national crisis and no greater sin than disloyalty to one's comrades in a time of war.

In addition to his knowledge of the wartime exploits of his fam-ily, his father was an encyclopedia of war and battles and the imple-ments of war. He knew the total tonnage of bombs dropped during every battle and the number of dead and wounded. He knew the implements of war, from artillery to pistols, and the impact each piece of ordnance had on victims. With the precision of an expert, he described the M-14 assault rifle, which had replaced the M-1 Garand of World War II and Korea, the M-79 grenade launcher, the M-60 machine gun, and the most reliable, the .50-caliber M-2 machine gun mounted on World War II bombers and tanks.

Dan once heard his father explaining the effects of napalm to Noah. "It's a mixture of petrol and a chemical that makes a tough sticky gel that attaches itself to the skin," his father said gravely. "Now you got to understand, boy, that napalm melts the flesh. Turns it to liquid so it melts down a man's face onto his chest and sits there, growing like a tumor outside the body. You know what I mean? The guy can't turn his head, because his throat and chest are packed so thick with flesh."

Dan would never forget that night because it was the first time Molly had harshly and openly criticized his father.

"It's sickening and unnatural!" she said angrily to Dan in their bedroom. "Noah sits there listening to him, hour after hour. It's like your father has him hypnotized!"

"Dad's just a good storyteller," Dan said. "He's able to make history vivid and real."

"Then let him write a book!" Molly cried. He's so proud of all the Scotts who have fought and died in all our wars, he should write a book! It might become a best-seller and he could appear on Leno or Letterman and tell his bloodthirsty stories to millions!"

"You know he can't write," Dan spoke quietly in an effort to calm her. "He's an oral storyteller."

"Then why don't you help him? If you spent more time with him, he'd have less time spilling his blood and guts to Noah!"

He understood her anger had to wear itself out, and they settled into the bed. Molly picked up the book she had been reading, and he reached for the *Nation* magazine from the bed stand. Pretending to be reading, from time to time he sneaked a look at her face in profile. He remembered thinking then how beautiful she had been as a young girl and how lovely she still was in her maturity. Her soft, fine hair was the shade of chestnuts, and she wore it cut short to reveal her small, shapely ears. He loved her dearly, and it distressed him to see her anger and heartache.

After a while, Dan turned off his lamp. "Goodnight, hon."

"Goodnight." Molly's voice was low and still troubled.

A few moments later his wife closed her lamp. They lay in silence in the darkened room, the wind lightly rattling the sash of the window. Somewhere on the stillness of their small-town street, the Harvis family dog barked.

"I know it's not fair for me to take my resentment and bile out on you," Molly's voice carried softly in the darkness. "I know how much your father loves Noah, and I know he means well. But this has been going on for years all through Noah's childhood. When he should have been listening to fairy tales, your father has been telling him of wars and of the Scotts who fought and died in them."

"Noah has always been interested in battles and wars," Dan said. "As a boy, remember how excited he became when we first read the *Iliad*? He was fascinated with Achilles and Hector and their battle before the walls of Troy. I read the *Iliad* to him a half dozen times, and he continued reading it himself when he grew older."

"Every boy has an inherent attraction to war," Molly said with resignation. "It goes with the male gender from the time primitive men bashed in the skulls of other primitive men. Some of that appeal is inevitable, but your father has fanned and nourished these feelings in Noah. You know I love the old man, but in my heart I can't forgive him for what he's done to Noah."

He had no answer he could offer to reassure her, and he turned and gently slipped his arm around Molly's waist, the way they had slept when they first married.

When Dan finally left his car and entered the high school, the corridors were thronged with young people, their jubilant faces and laughing voices a reminder that his son had once been a student in these same classrooms. In those years, when they had passed one another in the hallways, Noah would give his father a quick, playful wink. On a few occasions they had eaten lunch together in the cafeteria, but for the most part, Dan preferred that his son associate with his own friends. Now, with Noah so far away, despite knowing his feelings were selfish, he couldn't help envying the parents of other young people who had their sons and daughters living safely at home.

He went first to his small, book-strewn and paper-littered office to pick up assignments he had graded, then walked to the teacher's lounge for a cup of coffee. He greeted several other teachers who were also having coffee before beginning their classes.

"What do you hear from Noah?" Sue Norris, an older, white-haired English teacher, asked.

"He's doing all right," Dan said cheerfully. "We had a letter from him last week."

"He's in my prayers each night," the teacher said gravely.

"Thank you, Sue."

On the way to his first class, the principal, Benjamin Sloan, stopped him in the corridor to ask about Noah. When Noah first left for the Marines, Sloan had posted his photograph on the bulletin board in his office, and it hung there still. Dan reassured the principal that his son's letters remained optimistic.

He entered his morning honors literature class, which held about twenty seniors, evenly divided between boys and girls. He enjoyed seeing their handsome faces and sharing in their high spirits. As they were settling into their desks, Kevin Boyer asked him about Noah.

"He's doing all right, Kevin," Dan said. "We had a good letter from him just the other day."

"My cousin, Leo, who lives in Crown Point, is in Iraq too," Debbie Fairfield said. "He wrote his family that the suicide bombings were getting worse."

"My father said that when our soldiers can train more Iraqis, things will get better," Rick Emerson said.

"They should send over more troops and kick some butt!"

"What they should do is bring our soldiers home! Let the Iraqis fight for their own country!"

Dan stood beside his own desk, waiting until his students quieted down and settled into their seats. Art Brown threw a wadded piece of paper at Debbie Fairfield, who turned to glare at him.

"Art, pick that paper up, please," Dan said quietly. "Try to remember you're a senior now. That kind of kid stuff belongs back in grade school."

"Sorry, Mr. Scott. I just got carried away." The student grinned.

"Keep up your foolishness and you'll carry yourself right into an extra assignment you can do over the weekend."

He opened the textbook they had been studying.

"Today, we'll continue our assessment of *The Trojan Women* by the Greek tragedian Euripides," Dan said. "As we discussed yesterday, the play begins sometime after Homer's story in the *Iliad* ends, with the fall of Troy to the Greeks. *The Trojan Women* was first produced as a play in the year 415, after the Athenians had launched a barbaric, unprovoked attack that destroyed the island of Melos. That island's only crime was its refusal to join the Athenian federation, and Athens decided to punish it brutally. After the destruction of Melos, Athens prepared an expedition to conquer Sicily and also force that island to join the Athenian Empire."

He noticed several students, perhaps catching scents of spring, staring out the windows.

"The playwright, Euripides, was sickened by the massacre his countrymen had inflicted on the people of Melos, slaughtering the men and boys and selling the women and children into slavery. He was also appalled by the brutal imperialism his fellow Athenians demonstrated as they prepared to launch a fleet to conquer Syracuse. That attack proved to be a disastrous defeat for Athens. Many young Athenian men were killed and many thousands more condemned to hard labor for the rest of their lives in the salt mines of Syracuse. The Greek historian Thucydides, in a single moving line, defined the fate of those young men. 'Having done what men could, they suffered what men must.'"

Pausing for a moment, Dan wondered how many of his students could comprehend the artful poignancy of the simple line that encompassed the terrible fate of those youths condemned to labor in the mines until their death.

"*The Trojan Women* picks up the story of Troy after the great Trojan warrior Hector has been killed by Achilles as retribution for the death of his comrade Patroclus. Troy has fallen and the war is over. Hector's mother, Hecuba, his wife, Andromache, and their infant son, Astyanax, have been captured by the Greeks. Knowing they are to be taken back to Greece as slaves, mother and grandmother hope the infant will be allowed to journey with them. But the Greek captains led by Agamemnon, king of Mycenae, fear that Astyanax may grow up to seek vengeance on the Greeks for his father's death, and they order the boy killed."

He paused.

"I gave you an assignment yesterday to read the play and mark a brief section that you'd like to read to the class. Since the characters in *The Trojan Women* are principally women, I'll select several girls to read the passages. Who would like to start?"

Half a dozen girls raised their hands, and he selected Audi Craven, a pretty blonde girl who was the daughter of Matt Craven, owner of the town's Buick agency.

Audi stood up, holding the open book in her hands.

"I've chosen the passage where Hector's wife grieves over the death of her husband." The girl began to read.

> "And light words and gay
> Parley of women never passed my door.
> The thoughts of my own heart—I craved no more—
> Spake with me and I was happy. Constantly
> I brought fair silence and a tranquil eye
> For Hector's greeting, and watched well the way
> Of living, where to guide and where to obey.
> O my Hector, best beloved."

"C'mon, Audi, how come you never say anything like that to me?" Michael Whalen, a handsome, swaggering youth and a fullback on the Provincefield Cougars football team, interrupted with a smirk.

The class burst into laughter. Dan gestured brusquely for silence.

"You'd do better, Mike, if you'd spend more time reading the play and less time opening your mouth when you're not supposed to speak," he said. "That might just help bring your grades out of what Euripides called 'that cave of darkness where no light breaks.'"

His comment provoked another round of laughter.

"Sorry, Mr. Scott," the boy said, but his face denied repentance.

"Go ahead, Audi," Dan said. The girl resumed her reading.

> "That being mine, wast all in all to me,
> My prince, my wise one, O my majesty
> Of valiance!
> No man's touch had ever come
> Near me, when thou from out my father's home

Didst lead me and make me thine . . . And thou art
 dead.
And I war-flung to slavery and the bread
Of shame."

The girl articulated the words of the play clearly but in a flat, static voice indicating she had no comprehension of the emotions the scene involved.

Dan wondered how many of the class related the destruction of Troy to the war in Iraq. As they studied the Greek tragedies with their tales of rulers driven by arrogance into disastrous adventures, he had made casual references to Iraq, hoping to provoke some manner of discussion. But his students were unable to discern any parallels between the actions of their own government and those of the rulers of ancient Athens. Dan resisted pressing the comparison for fear the scorn Euripides had felt toward Athenian imperialism might reveal Dan's own revulsion toward the Bush administration and the war in which his son and other young American men and women were fighting. His criticism was also muted by the awareness that if the senseless war continued even a few more years, young men like Mike Whalen might end up fighting there.

"Good reading, Audi," he said. "Who else wishes to read a passage?"

From the few hands that fluttered in the air, he selected Melinda Fielding, one of his better students. She was a thin, plain-faced girl, burdened by having barely any breasts, somehow always isolated from the ebullient camaraderie of the class. Dan remembered meeting her mother once in a parent-teacher conference, a woman as gloomy as her daughter, evoking melancholy even before she spoke.

"I've selected the passage where Queen Hecuba grieves for her grandson, Astyanax, who has been thrown from the walls to his death by the Greeks," Melinda said. "The passage begins as the queen takes the broken, dead body of her grandson into her arms."

In a clear, solemn voice, the girl began to read.

"Ah, what a death hath found thee, little one! . . .
Ye tender arms, the same dear mold have ye
As your father . . . And dear proud lips, so full of hope.
And closed forever!"

From the very first lines she read, it was evident the girl had a lucid and chilling understanding of the old queen's anguish. Slowly, the emotional intensity her voice and feeling provided the words compelled the restless class to silence.

> "What false words ye said
> At daybreak when ye crept into my bed,
> Called me kind names and promised, 'Grandmother,
>   When thou art dead, I will cut close my hair
> And lead out all the captains to ride by
> Thy tomb.'"

Dan felt the haunting power in the girl's reading, her voice evoking the landscape of the ruined city with its crumbled towers, burial smoke spiraling into the sky, while the grieving women mourned the death of the young prince. In his own readings of the play, he had never before experienced the emotion he felt at that moment, a sorrow so deep and profound that it pierced his heart.

> "Why didst thou cheat me so? 'Tis I,
> Old, homeless, childless, that for me must shed
> Cold tears, so young, so miserably dead."

And as the girl who understood loneliness and had experience of despair ended her reading, Dan turned away quickly to conceal from his class the tears that burned in his eyes. In that moment, he comprehended how human suffering had remained unchanged from the time of Troy: sorrow the same, mourning the same. In the lament of the old queen, he grasped once again the anguish of parents and grandparents who endured their children's deaths, untimely deaths, violating the cycle of the generations wherein children lived to bury their parents.

He turned back to the class.

"A wonderful and dramatic reading, Melinda!" Dan said earnestly. "You truly made us feel and understand Queen Hecuba's grief."

A smile of pleasure and gratefulness brightened the young girl's face.

Chapter 2

DAN HAD RECOLLECTIONS OF HIS FATHER THAT DID NOT involve battles and wars. These memories belonged to his childhood and to Hammond, a city at the Indiana state line neighboring Chicago, where he had been born and had grown up. The city had been named after George Hammond, owner of a large slaughterhouse, the first industry to locate in the area. In 1869, Hammond began packing beef in ice-filled railroad cars for shipment to the East, ending forever the shipping of live cattle by rail.

Dan's father worked as a mill foreman in the U.S. Steel Works in Gary. His family lived in a neat frame house beside other neat frame houses on a street barren of trees or shrubs. On the corner, occupying the space of a dozen houses, was a rectory, an ornate example of Romanesque Revival architecture. Dan would stand outside the black wrought-iron fence surrounding the rectory, waiting to catch a glimpse of the Roman Catholic priest. The cleric's somber demeanor and black garb suggested to Dan that he ruled witches and demons inhabiting the rectory.

In the evening, as they waited for his father to return from work, his mother prepared dinner and Dan set dishes and silver on the kitchen table. Other steelworkers often stopped to have a few drinks in one of the numerous neighborhood taverns, but his father was always eager to get home. Dan knew almost to the minute when he'd hear his father's heavy tread on the back porch, and a moment later his large, broad frame would fill the doorway.

"Thomas Joshua Scott is home!" his strong voice would boom through the kitchen. He'd kiss his wife gently and then hug his son. Dan remembered his father's clothing smelling of the sulfur and ash of the mills.

"Spike Ferris, he's the burner I've told you about before, tore his Achilles tendon at the mill today."

"An accident in the mill?" his mother asked.

"Nothing to do with the mill," his father grinned. "The yahoo slipped off the edge of the desk he was sitting on in the scheduler's office. They had to take him to the hospital." He winked at Dan.

"You ever hear anything so damn foolish? A steelworker injuring himself falling off a desk!"

At least twice a week his mother prepared his father's favorite meal, home-baked ham coated with brown sugar, lima beans, and thickly sliced full-grained wheat bread. For a beverage, his father drank a large glass of dark-bodied beer. Dan never saw his father drink a glass of wine, just as he never saw his mother drink a glass of beer.

Dan remembered his mother as a lovely woman, tall and stately with fine, delicate features. She had been born of a Boston patrician family, her father a banker, her mother a distant relative of the venerable Cabots. From snatches of conversation between his parents, Dan understood that his mother's family had not approved of her marriage.

His paternal grandparents had both died when he was very small. He saw his maternal grandparents on several occasions in his childhood, when his mother took him east to visit. They would ride a train, eat sandwiches and fruit she had packed, and sleep overnight in their seats.

In Boston, his grandparent's house—as large as the rectory on their corner in Hammond—had a great winding stairway to the second floor and a maze of rooms. They ate dinner at a long table in the dining room that could seat thirty to forty people. Although he was curious as to how the kitchen compared to their own small one in Hammond, Dan never saw beyond the door from which servants emerged to bring them food.

His grandfather was tall, as reserved as Dan's father was boisterous, with long sideburns. In contrast to the smell of the mill his father's clothing carried, his grandfather smelled of strong cigars. His grandmother was as tall as his mother, gray-haired, and she wore a great brooch at her throat. When they left after what would be the last time he saw her, she kissed him on the forehead and gave him a silver dollar.

The visits were stiff and uncomfortable, everyone speaking quietly, and Dan was always grateful to get back to their warm, cozy kitchen and the table that comfortably seated three. Despite the disparity in their backgrounds, he never doubted that his father and mother loved each other very much. His father's exuberant temperament balanced the quiet steadfastness of his mother's nature. As Dan grew older, he came to understand that his mother was the compass around which his father directed his life.

As his father would recount one of his wartime stories to a group of friends, his big hands chopping the air, a range of expressions would be visible on his face. He'd savor the words, anticipating the effect they'd have on his listeners before allowing them to emerge from between his teeth. Dan's mother would sit quietly watching him, listening as she must have listened to the same stories a hundred times. Sometimes Dan detected a faint crease of a smile in her cheeks, a smile that he understood wasn't mockery or condescension but resulted from the pleasure one takes watching a gifted child perform. Above all, her face radiated the enormity of her love.

Dan thought it an unhappy coincidence that his mother—as would later be true for his wife—had suffered two miscarriages before Dan was born. Both he and Noah were solitary sons.

"The three of us," he recalled his father saying at their kitchen table, "my little family." Dan saw the corners of his eyes red and moist while an awkward effort at a smile trembled on his lips. "By God, that's all I want and all I'll ever need!"

Yet, as Dan grew older, he heard his mother express remorse because she hadn't been able to give his father the large family he had wanted, the family he had spoken of desiring in their early years, "three daughters and three sons!"

Although Dan was a solitary child and could not remember having any close friends as he grew up, his childhood memories weren't unhappy. He would descend the steps of their house and walk past the ornate rectory toward the railroad yards a couple of blocks farther away. He'd sit on a bench and watch the great black engines whistling and puffing, shunting and banging around cars. When a train had been formed and started from the yards, the monstrous black engine dragged a seemingly endless span of freight cars with the names of assorted railroads blazoned on the sides. The red and white caboose, rocking from side to side, would bring up the rear.

His mother had introduced him to the magic of the library not far from their house. He loved the smell and feel of books and would walk out proudly with several of them under his arm. When they got home, his mother would read the stories to him in her fine, modulated voice until he was able to read them for himself.

Because of the absence of trees on their street, the hot summer sun came burning down upon the unshielded houses, and the winter snow piled in thick mounds upon the roof. But he also had an unobstructed view of the sunsets that he watched with fascination from the large bay window. As twilight fell, he saw over the roofs of other houses a band of black, crested by scarlet, and, above that, a crown of brighter red. Meanwhile, drifting clouds created the shapes of animals against the yellow sky.

There was another memory Dan had of his father, an event that transpired the year he was to enter high school. On one of his walks home, he had been accosted by a half dozen youths about his own age. He had heard of neighborhood gangs but hadn't met any of them before. The leader of the boys, a lean, hard-eyed youth with unkempt hair, reached out and caught Dan's arm.

"Where you live, boy?"

"Over on Locust."

"You want to join our gang, boy?" the leader asked, his voice deceptively soft.

Dan stood there mute, his breathing tense in his chest, a flutter of trembling in his knees.

"Who in hell wants this pansy in the gang, Crow?" one of the others said.

The leader looked at Dan and smiled, showing several stained, yellow teeth. "You a pansy, boy?" The youth's grip on his shoulders became tighter, and he knew they meant to hurt him. "We don't like pansies. When we find a pansy, we teach him a lesson so's he won't forget us."

Dan made an effort to pull away, but Crow's grip on his arm grew more painful. His heart pounded harder.

At that moment he saw the bulk of his father turn the corner and start toward them. Something in the way Thomas Scott walked conveyed a threat to the youths, and Crow released Dan's arm.

His father came closer, his bulky jacket making him appear even bigger and more formidable. He walked past Dan and put his big hand on Crow's shoulder. A taunting smile creased his lips.

"You the big yahoo here, boy?" his father asked.

Crow stared at him without speaking.

"Now I don't know what you yahoos were planning," his father said, his voice grave and measured, "but this here is my son. Wherever he walks in this neighborhood, he's under my protection. If any of you ever lays a hand on him, I'll come after you. You understand? I mean I'll come find each of you in your houses and I'll kick the living shit out of you. And if your fathers or brothers get in my way, I'll kick the shit out of them, as well. You understand what I'm saying?"

The youths stared at Thomas Scott, and several mumbled a cowed assent. His father let Crow go with a slight, contemptuous push. He turned to Dan.

"We better get home, son," he said. "Your mom will have dinner ready."

That had been Dan's first and only encounter with Crow and his gang.

When he became a sophomore at Jefferson High School, Dan dated a few Polish and German girls from the neighborhood whose fathers also worked in the mills. The first girl he ever kissed was a plump German girl named Helga, who had a lovely face and wore her long blonde tresses in braids. But he was never really drawn to any girl until Molly.

They met when both were seniors, Molly attending school in Provincefield and Dan in Hammond. She had been one of the cheerleaders at a basketball game between their schools and was easily the prettiest and most vivacious girl on the squad. Dan maneuvered himself from his seat high in the stands, coming closer to the court to get a better glimpse of her. For the remainder of that game, the action on the court interested him less than the vision of the lovely young girl, cheering and prancing, her short cheerleader's skirt flouncing provocatively around her slender legs.

Conscious of feeling awkward and ill at ease, he mustered the boldness to speak to her after the game. She seemed to overlook his shyness, and they arranged to meet the following weekend. That began a relationship that lasted during the balance of their senior year and through the summer following their graduations.

He used his father's Ford pickup or his mother's Honda to drive from Hammond to Provincefield so he and Molly could spend a few hours together.

In the fall, Molly entered Purdue University and Dan went to the University of Indiana. Although both of them solemnly agreed the sensible thing to do was date others, they exchanged letters and, during the summers, resumed their relationship. After finishing work at his summer job at the Shell station in Hammond, Dan would drive to Provincefield. Sometimes on Sunday afternoons Molly would drive to Hammond to meet him. The bond between them grew stronger, and when they became seniors they made a decision to marry after they graduated. Molly's father and mother and his own parents approved of their union and felt them to be a good match.

"I like that girl," his father told him brusquely once after Molly had eaten Sunday dinner with them. "There isn't any nonsense about her. You'll always know where you stand with her, and she'll never let you down. You take her, son, before some other yahoo sees those same qualities and steals her away."

They were married in Molly's church in Provincefield. A group of his father's friends came from the steel mill, and the celebration became a little rowdy. But Dan and Molly didn't mind, marveling at the bond that now linked them. They looked forward to their life together.

After their marriage, they lived for a while with her parents in Provincefield where Molly's father was a pharmacist. Dan studied for his teaching certificate and applied for a position as a teacher at Provincefield High School. The year he was accepted and began to teach, Molly's father died of a heart attack, and her mother decided to move to Canton, Ohio, to live with Molly's brother. At that time, Molly and Dan inherited her mother's house. It was while they lived in that house that, after Molly's two miscarriages, Noah was born. After they learned Molly could not conceive any more children, they were grateful that this son had survived.

Although Dan spoke of returning to graduate school for an advanced degree that would qualify him to teach at a university, the years slipped by with distressing speed. Molly worked at the Heart Center and Dan at the high school. His work provided him a certain fulfillment because he felt he was contributing to the education and development of young people. Molly also felt a satisfaction in her profession because she was a talented therapist who was also compassionate toward the heart patients with whom she worked. Their lives settled into a certain routine, and they were as happy as any man and wife enduring daily travail could be. Dan loved his wife dearly and felt her love for him was just as strong. Their love fostered an even more bountiful love they lavished on their son.

In the early 1990s, Dan's mother died. She'd been suffering from cancer for almost a year, and the chemotherapy she undertook as treatment made her weak and frail. He and Molly visited her a couple of times a week, often taking Noah with them.

When she realized she had only a short time to live, his mother had insisted on being moved to the hospice, despite his father's pleas that she remain at home so he might continue looking after her. Her body, even wasting and expiring, emanated that same fragrance of lavender Dan always remembered. Sometimes in a crowd, he'd catch that fragrance worn by a woman, and it returned him to a memory of his mother.

On what was their final visit, while Molly sat in an anteroom with Noah and his father, Dan sat beside his mother's bed and held her hand. Even as he grieved at the thought of losing her, he marveled at the way she accepted her imminent death with the same grace and dignity she had lived her life. That night his mother spoke to him for the last time.

"Look after your father," she said softly. The faintest trace of a smile trembled at the corner of her lips. "But don't expect to do too much with him. He's a willful man."

The few words she spoke had exhausted her. Her final words only trembled on her lips, no sound emerging, but he knew she was saying, "I love you . . ."

She died later that evening while Dan and his father stood on either side of her bed, each holding one of her hands. Her eyes, partly lidded, shaded by the nearness of death, gazed at his father.

In those final moments, Dan witnessed his father's great will and courage that enabled him to endure the carnage of war, battling to hold his wife to life. Finally, a look of recognition and acceptance passed between them, a look that consummated the life they had lived together. Dan saw them joined in a final farewell that excluded him and everything else in the world.

In the final few years leading up to the millennium, changes had come to Provincefield. As with other small towns within driving distance of Chicago, acres of farmland had been sold to erect large housing developments. New, upgraded railroad cars were added to the old South Shore Electric line, which had served the region for decades. At the perimeter of the town, a series of mini-malls had been built that included a new Jewel and K-Mart as well as a McDonald's and a Kentucky Fried Chicken. A Holiday Inn and a Super 8 Motel had also been erected.

While Provincefield no longer had a train station, the maze of tracks still running through the town led one inhabitant to say, "Our banks are the safest in the Midwest. Any fleeing bank robber would be sure to be blocked by a long freight passing through one of the intersections."

Despite the changes, the culture and customs of the small town remained much the same. People interacted with one another not based on social status or bank balances but on the nature and character of the individual. Residents lived more organically connected than was possible in larger cities. Friendships formed in high school remained durable into marriages and the birth of children. There was an almost obsessive focus on sports, most of the town celebrating a victory of its high school team and lamenting its defeats. A score of shops in town posted the schedules of Provincefield's basketball, track, and football teams. But the town wasn't only sports-oriented: the residents were also proud that their high school debating team had twice won national titles.

During football season, when Noah had starred in a game against some rival team, congratulations were offered to Dan.

"Great game your boy played last night, Dan!" one of the townspeople might say. "That last scramble of his was something to see! If he wanted to, I bet after college he could finish up with a pro team like the Colts or the Bears."

If the Cougars lost to their opponents, the townspeople offered their sympathy.

"Our boys, including Noah, played a great game, but that Panther quarterback was too sharp. The son-of-a-gun never missed his target."

Celebrations and sorrows were shared. When Peter and Clair Pifko's son was married, several neighbors, including Dan and Molly, opened their houses to wedding guests from out-of-town. And the entire block celebrated.

In August of 1999, when the Bukowskis, who lived four houses away from Molly and Dan, lost their eight-year-old daughter after she was struck and killed by a delivery truck, a pall of sorrow settled over the street. For days afterward, voices and activity all along their block were muted.

Dan understood that to many of the students at the high school, Provincefield, like other small towns, was a barren settlement, forever unchanging and out of touch with modern life. He understood their yearning to burst their shackles and leave town to begin what they felt would be more fruitful lives elsewhere.

But he loved the small town where they lived. He was grateful each time he entered their comfortable house situated on a street with many pines and oaks, trees verdant with leafage in the spring and colorfully burnished foliage in the autumn. He savored the silence along the street at night, the wind rustling through the trees outside their bedroom windows. The trains that delayed traffic during the daylight hours became friendlier at night, harbingers of nostalgia as their plaintive whistles carried him back to the nights of his childhood when his dreams seemed boundless.

As in many midwestern towns, the politics in Provincefield tended to be conservative, most of the residents voting Republican. For the most part, however, Democrats and Republicans and a handful of fringe party candidates lived in mutual tolerance of one another's beliefs.

Dan and Molly had always been Democrats. Thomas Scott had voted Democrat as well in earlier elections, but the conduct of Bill Clinton with the young intern in the White House had soured him on the party.

"You shouldn't blame the Democrats for the actions of a single man, even if he's president," Dan said to his father.

"A sour apple can spoil the whole barrel," his father said gravely.

"What he did with that young girl was mean and dishonorable. He's made our nation a laughingstock before the world. If his party loses in the upcoming election, a lot of it will be his fault."

The general tolerance for others' beliefs came under strain in the bitterly contested election of 2000, which pitted Republicans George Bush and Dick Cheney against Democrats Al Gore and Joe Lieberman. Television commercials run by both parties were spiteful and rancorous, as were the debates that came near the end of the campaign.

While Molly and Dan were also disappointed at the reprehensible conduct of the charismatic and able president, there was nothing about the Republican Party or its policies that would induce them to change their allegiance.

The closeness of the November 7 election and the uncertainty of the outcome produced a tension in their town and across the country that lasted for weeks as the Florida results were disputed. When Bush won the Florida vote by a little over a 1,000 votes, Florida law provided for an automatic recount. The final, hotly disputed official Florida count gave the victory to Bush by 537 votes. But the Gore campaign claimed that many ballots remained uncounted.

In the vindictive barrage of complaints and counter-complaints that followed, the Bush campaign filed suit against the manual recounts. Numerous local courts ruled both ways, some ordering recounts and others claiming recounts were superfluous. The Florida Supreme Court ordered the recounting process to proceed. In the beginning of December, the Bush campaign appealed to the Supreme Court of the United States. On December 12 of that year, about five weeks after the election, the U.S. Supreme Court handed down a ruling in favor of Bush by a 5–4 vote, ending the legal reviews.

On the evening of December 13, 2000, Dan, Molly, Thomas Scott, and Noah had listened to Al Gore concede that he had lost the election.

"He's a good man," Thomas Scott said somberly. "He's putting the good of the country before his own party and his personal ambitions."

"It was one of the most vindictive and spiteful election campaigns I've ever seen," Molly said bitterly. "In the end, the Democrats were robbed." She rose and walked, still agitated, from the room.

"Mom's a tough nut," Noah grinned. "She won't forgive or forget."

"Don't let me hear you say a word about your mother," Thomas Scott said sternly. "Jenny and I knew the first time we ever met her that she was a champion. She was the luckiest thing ever happened to your father."

In the years after Thomas Scott had come to live with Dan and Molly, their house became a visitor's attraction. Everyone in Provincefield soon learned of the exploits of Thomas Scott, and they treated him like a celebrity. During the summer months, he'd sit in his oversized rocking chair on the front porch, and townspeople would stop by to chat and listen to his stories.

Dan knew that Molly found the endless repetition of the stories and the constant presence of people wearisome, but she never complained and went out of her way to accommodate the visitors. When she was home, she'd carry out a jug of lemonade or, on hot days, offer guests cold cans of beer.

But Noah found the presence of visitors paying his grandfather homage exciting and justified. When he came home from school, he'd often sit with his grandfather on the porch, relishing the effect Thomas Scott's wartime stories had on the listeners. He once said proudly to his parents that "Gramps makes us just about the most famous people in town!"

Sometimes Noah brought a few of his friends from high school and they clustered around Thomas Scott while Noah implored his grandfather to tell them the "story of the landing at Omaha Beach." Thriving on the audience, Thomas Scott would tell the story with relish, punctuating the tale with an occasional "goddamn" or "sonofabitch" and slapping his knee with his big hand.

The highlight of the year for both grandfather and grandson were the Memorial Day festivities. The town would celebrate enthusiastically with many flags displayed outside houses and on the town hall and police station. The Provincefield High School band would rehearse "The Star-Spangled Banner" and "The Battle Hymn of the Republic" for weeks. His father would pull out his old World War II uniform, which a seamstress had opened several times to accommodate his added weight. The rugged, gray-haired man, his chest emblazoned with his medals and ribbons, made an impressive sight. As a child cradled between his grandfather's knees and later seated in a chair beside Thomas Scott, Noah shared in the admiration and praise that his grandfather received at these events. Other veterans brought their families to greet the most famous veteran among them, Thomas "Tracker" Scott, decorated for exceptional valor during the landing at Omaha Beach.

With his son enamored of Thomas Scott's charisma, Dan felt himself in his father's shadow. He was a teacher, ink in his veins instead of blood. It wasn't that he didn't have a good relationship with Noah, but his father had a better one. Even as Dan urged his father to continue living with them, he breathed a sigh of relief when his father decided it was time for him to move to the Veterans' Home.

In the first year of the Bush administration, September 11 occurred. Dan was at school and Molly at work when the news broke. Both at the high school and at the Heart Center, students, staff, and patients gathered around television sets. The networks played and replayed the spectacle of the first plane striking one of the World Trade Center Towers and then the second. For a few moments after the first strike, broadcasters assumed it to be an accident. When another plane struck the second tower, the dimensions of the catastrophe became apparent. There was uncertainty as to whether a foreign power had launched a war against the United States. All commercial air travel was frozen, and planes already in the air were ordered to land at the nearest airport. Word came from Washington that the president, vice president, and members of the cabinet had been rushed away to secret locations.

After September 11, terrorism became the principal topic of conversation on the television and in the print media. Airport security became more stringent, and within weeks the Patriot Act was introduced and quickly passed in Congress.

The year Noah was a junior in high school, Thomas Scott's physical afflictions grew more severe. He was eighty-six years old, a big, muscular man whose body had added some weight over the years. If he became handicapped and unable to care for himself, no one in their house would be able to move him. As decisively as he had made decisions in combat, Dan's father resolved to move to the Veterans' Home in Cranston, about ten miles from Provincefield. Both Dan and Molly made an effort to convince him to remain with them, but he was too proud a man to stay and have them dragging him around.

"You been looking after me real good now in the years since I moved in with you," he said firmly. "I couldn't have gotten more loving care in any other family. Now that my bum back and splintered hips make it harder and harder for me to walk, I know, before long, I'm going into a wheelchair. It's the right time for me to join the other old troopers in the Home. I'll be fine. You remember when we visited Joe Feltzer there? Why, they got doctors right on the premises and dentists and eye doctors, too. They even got one of those urinary plumbers coming in regularly. Hell, I been going to doctors' offices for so many years, let them come to me now. I put in my service for my country; now let my country look after me." He paused and winked. "Besides, you know how much I like telling stories, so I'll sit around sharing war tales with the other inmates and we'll see who can tell the biggest lies."

Although they did not speak of it to one another, Dan knew that Molly was as relieved as he at his father's decision to leave the house. Although his father had not been demanding or troublesome, his very presence through the years had overshadowed their lives. When they had friends in for dinner, Thomas Scott's aura of heroism dominated the table. Before long, in response to a question one of the guests would ask about his medals or his service, Thomas Scott had taken over the conversation, telling stories of the wars in which the Scotts had participated. Even as Dan understood that their guests genuinely enjoyed his father's stories, it stifled or deflected any other conversation.

Noah was the person in their house most devastated by Thomas Scott's planned departure. When they told him his grandfather was moving to the Veterans' Home, tears of frustration and anger made their son's voice tremble.

"Why should he leave! This has been his home since Granny died! Why does he have to leave?"

"Noah, we tried to keep him here," Molly said. "Both your dad and I pleaded with him. But it was his decision. He's a man who in a few more years will be ninety. He has the right to make up his own mind."

"You should have tried harder to convince him!" Noah cried. "This is his home! This is where he belongs so we can look after him! If he needed to be carried around, I'd do it! You know I'm strong enough to do it! I promise you that every hour I'm not in school or working, I'd look after him so he wouldn't be any bother to either of you!"

"You know your grandfather," Dan said, his son's pleas filling him with remorse because he had not tried harder to get his father to remain. "You know how proud he is and how he doesn't want to be a burden to anyone. Nobody could make your grandfather do anything he doesn't want to do. After all, he'll be only ten miles away. We'll visit him regularly and bring him home for visits anytime he wishes. Besides, here in our house, he spent a lot of time alone while your mom and I worked and you were in school. In the home he'll have people around all the time, other veterans with whom he can share stories."

Despite their explanations, Noah protested his grandfather leaving until the day of Thomas Scott's departure. Then he drove with Dan and his grandfather to the Veterans' Home. Dan and Noah saw Thomas Scott through admittance and walked with him to his quarters, a small but clean and neat room with windows looking across a courtyard and a garden.

"Will you look at this?" Thomas Scott said with what Dan recognized was a charade of delight for Noah's sake. "My own bed and bathroom and a view to boot! Hell, this is even better than I had back in your house! And I'll have that pretty nurse you saw in the hallway looking after me!"

"Remember, next weekend the Cougars will be playing Gary," Noah said. "We'll come and get you so you can watch the game."

"Sure, you can! You think I want to miss my grandson's glory on the field? I'll be there with bells on!"

Dan said good-bye to his father, and then, knowing Noah and

his father wanted their farewell to be private, he waited for his son in the foyer.

Noah remained inconsolably silent on their drive home. Several times Dan tried to engage him in conversation.

"It's really a nice looking place, don't you think?" Dan asked. "It's clean, and the staff, the nurses, and attendants seem pleasant. There will always be a doctor nearby if one is needed. I'm sure he'll be fine."

Noah had his head turned away, staring out the window at the farmland they passed, and said nothing. Dan felt his son's reproach in his silence.

Even after Thomas Scott was gone, his presence in the house remained, his voice lingering, his stories repeated so often they served to keep his magnetism alive. Fearing they might be stolen or lost in the Veterans' Home, Thomas Scott had left most of the Scott family decorations, including the two Medals of Honor, in the room he had occupied in Dan and Molly's house. The small glass cases enclosing medals and ribbons won for valor by generations of Scotts adorned the walls, along with several regimental battle flags. Sometimes in the evenings, Noah spent as much time reading and studying in his grandfather's room as he did in his own.

Several times a week, Noah took Dan's truck or Molly's car and visited his grandfather. In the beginning, on several occasions, Dan went with him and witnessed the rampant pride his father took in Noah, who wheeled him around the corridors.

"This here's my grandson," Thomas Scott would say proudly to any group of veterans he passed. "You ever seen a handsomer kid? Takes after his grandmother and mother, both of them beauties. And you should see what he can do on a football field! Best running back the Provincefield Cougars ever had and probably the best in the whole Midwest! But the boy's not only athletic, he's smart too! Straight A's last semester! What do you think of that?"

Tagging along behind his son and father, feeling useless and barely noticed, Dan stopped visiting at the same time Noah went. Dan saw his father twice a week, but Noah went to the Veterans' Home even more often. While other youths spent hours during the weekends with their friends, lounging around the local ice cream or fast food shops, Noah drove to visit his grandfather as soon as he finished his shift at the Kentucky Fried Chicken restaurant.

When Noah's friends visited him in their home, he'd take them into his grandfather's room and show them the Medals of Honor and tell them the stories about Shiloh and the Second Battle of the Marne, the tank action at Chonju, and the landings at Omaha Beach.

Once when Molly suggested that they convert Thomas Scott's room into a guest room, removing his assorted decorations and battle flags from the walls and storing them safely away, Noah protested vehemently.

"Gramps will be coming back to visit for a few days over the holidays!" Noah said. "Where would he stay?"

"He could still sleep in the room. It just wouldn't have to remain a war museum if an overnight guest slept there."

"It's not a war museum!" Noah's voice carried an undertone of outrage. "It's a history of our family, of the Scotts and what they accomplished! Why would you want to hide all that away in a trunk?" Under the ferocity of Noah's reprimand, Molly gave in, and the room remained as it had been when Thomas Scott lived in it.

Although Dan would not admit it, even to Molly, he felt envious of his father's memories, of his heroism and his decorations, envious of the esteem in which Thomas Scott was held by his grandson. Sometimes, despite his own loathing at the idea of killing another human being, he wished he had been a soldier himself, tempered in the fire of combat. But that wasn't the reality in which he lived. The truth was that, for as many years as he could remember, every time Noah looked at him, it was as if he were staring through him at the huge and dominating presence of his grandfather.

Chapter 3

IN THE MONTHS THAT FOLLOWED THE ATTACK on the World Trade Center, when more than 3,000 lives were lost, the Bush administration leveled accusations at three countries, Iraq, Iran, and North Korea, which the president described as an "axis of evil." The focus of his denunciations appeared to be Saddam

Hussein in Iraq, charging the dictator with concealing weapons of mass destruction. The drumbeats toward war began pounding.

"That man isn't satisfied with the reports of the weapons inspectors in Iraq," Molly said. "He and his hawks have made up their minds to go to war. We've got to do all we can to stop them!"

With each speech that the president made, it became clear that war was the administration's objective. The climax of months of haranguing and maneuvering came during a session at the United Nations when Secretary of State Colin Powell laid out the government's case in methodical fashion, his presentation bolstered by an imposing array of photographs and charts.

In conversations about the impending conflict that Dan had with his father at the Veterans' Home, Thomas Scott wasn't entirely supportive of the push to war.

"I'm not sure the brass in Washington have thought this through," he said. "It's easy to get into a fight, but sometimes it's damn hard to get out."

Yet, despite his reservations, Thomas Scott vowed unconditional support if the president made the decision to go to war.

"Once the first shots are fired and our troops go into action," he said, "the discussion is over, ended, kaput! We don't want to go through another mess like Vietnam with the goddamn protesters back home undercutting the troops. You know what a soldier in combat feels like when he hears that back home they're calling the war he's fighting in useless and criminal? I tell you it cuts out his heart!"

Dan and Molly were both actively against the country going into the war over the unproven presence of weapons of mass destruction in Iraq. Molly was especially vehement in her feelings that the cabal of men around Bush had an agenda of their own that they were hiding from the American people.

During dinner one night in the home of friends who were supportive of the government's actions, the conversation at the table grew heated.

"Saddam has proven he's capable of using chemical and biological weapons against his own people," said Walt Franklin, another high school teacher at whose house they were having dinner. "What do you think would stop him from using them against Israel or even against us?"

"That's ridiculous!" Molly snapped. "He used those weapons against unarmed Kurds who had no way of fighting back. That proves he's a butcher, but he's not a total fool. If he did have weapons of mass destruction, any move to use them against the U.S. or Israel would mean his destruction. We'd make Iraq a cemetery without a tree or house standing!"

"I wasn't totally convinced until I saw Colin Powell's presentation before the U.N.," Emily Franklin, Walt's wife, said. "But he demonstrated what seemed to be an airtight case."

"However good his case, it wouldn't hurt us to be a little patient and let the weapons inspectors complete their work," Dan said. "We've been able to contain Saddam Hussein for years now. Going to war should be a last resort."

"Those other countries in the U.N. are equivocating," Walt said. "Bush is right in wanting to bypass that ineffective debating society. We don't need permission from the U.N. to do what's best for our country."

"Goddamn it, you make me sick!" Molly cried. "How can going into a questionable war on a reckless and unfounded premise be what's best for our country?"

Walt and his wife were startled at Molly's outburst, and Dan looked at his wife in surprise. Despite their contrary political convictions, Walt and Emily were decent, sensitive people, and Molly had always enjoyed their company.

The conversation turned to less lethal topics, and after a while, Dan and Molly drove home.

"You were a little hard on Walt," Dan said during the drive.

"Fuck him and his drivel about what's best for the country," Molly said, her voice quivering with outrage. "He wouldn't be so goddamn eager for war if he had a son instead of two daughters."

Dan understood that the basis for Molly's agitation and anger was her concern for Noah. Even then she must have had a premonition of what might happen if the nation went to war.

The national debate on war continued. Pundits on the right and the left argued each side's case. The controversy no longer focused on whether Saddam Hussein had weapons of mass destruction but on how soon he planned to use them. Each of the president's speeches seemed to suggest an imminent, inescapable danger. Bush's heated rhetoric was echoed by Dick Cheney, Colin Powell, and National Security Advisor Condoleezza Rice in their appearances on the various talk shows. People rose each morning concerned that the deadly weapons in Saddam's hands might be launched against a U.S. target that very day.

Benjamin Sloan, the principal at the high school, a man whose opinions Dan respected, made the administration's case for war.

"The argument that Saddam Hussein used biological and chemical weapons only against his own unarmed citizens and wouldn't dare use them against us doesn't hold water," Sloan said to a group of his teachers during a discussion. "Hussein is a brutal ruler convinced of his own infallibility! We simply cannot count on his acting rationally! Look at Hitler's attack against Russia. He was warned by his entire general staff that any invasion into the Soviet heartland would prove a disaster. Hitler went against their advice and lost a war against the West he might otherwise have won."

Even if no one could be sure whether or not Saddam Hussein was hiding weapons of mass destruction, Dan believed the danger of nuclear weaponry extended far beyond Iraq. Iran and North Korea were both assumed to have nuclear programs in the works. As more and more countries obtained the bomb, the chances of one falling into the hands of some fanatical terrorist organization became more likely.

Dan wondered sometimes how people went about their daily work or were able to sleep at night with the frightful shadow of nuclear war hanging over their heads. He had read John Hershey's book on Hiroshima and remained chilled for days afterward at the destruction described in its pages. On that August day in 1945 when the B-29 named the *Enola Gay* dropped the uranium bomb, the people of Hiroshima suffered the apocalypse. The center of the blast burned at 5,400 degrees Fahrenheit—twice what was required to melt iron. The wind of blistering fire extended for miles. Three days later, the plutonium bomb was dropped on Nagasaki.

The people closest to the blast were vaporized instantly, sometimes leaving nothing behind but a silhouette on concrete. Those farther away had their eyes or intestines vacuumed out of their bodies at lightning speed. The men, women, and children burned by radiation found their bodies ballooned into chunks of distorted flesh. Many who were miles away from the blast were blinded. Even those who seemed to have escaped the effects of the bomb later had children born with organs outside their bodies or with stumps for legs and arms.

J. Robert Oppenheimer, the leading scientist on the Manhattan Project that created the bomb, described the detonation: "If the radiance of a thousand suns were to burst once into the sky, that would be like the splendor of the mighty one."

Later, haunted by the devastation the bomb had wrought and refusing to work on the hydrogen bomb, which would have 650 times the force of the earlier weapons, Oppenheimer quoted a line from Vishnu, from the Hindu scripture the Bhagavad Gita: "Now I am become Death, the destroyer of worlds."

Even if dropping the bombs could be justified as having saved tens of thousands of American soldiers who might have been killed in any invasion of Japan, the atomic age had begun, and the world would never be the same again. The nuclear age had been born, and for the first time in history, the magnitude of hate in men's hearts had found weapons to match.

Although Dan wasn't overly religious, he felt the biblical warnings about Armageddon had some validity. He feared for his own family and friends as well as for the families of others across his own country and even in the remainder of the world. That had to be the fear of any rational man or woman.

These fears and anxieties did not disturb him during the activity of the day but more often on nights when he couldn't sleep, his body suspended restlessly in silence and darkness. He had waking nightmares then of burned and devastated cities with deaths in such numbers that they rivaled the great plagues of history.

In those sleepless hours he could not help recalling with nostalgia the tranquillity of the nights he had spent as a child in his father and mother's house. His bed and room were sanctuaries then, secured by the comforting presence and protection of his parents.

Now, fearful that his country might provoke a war that could unleash those nuclear monsters, he signed petitions and wrote his congressman and senators even as he experienced feelings of futility at the inadequacy of those partial measures. He felt his efforts were the flutters of a snowflake in a blizzard.

Molly took a more aggressive stance against the impending war. She joined protest movements and, on several occasions, drove into Indianapolis or Chicago to participate in rallies against the war.

At an American Legion convention in Indianapolis, she had joined a group of women passing out leaflets condemning the belligerence of the Bush administration. She had driven home that evening, her dress stained with the eggs and tomatoes that had been hurled at her.

"They called me whore, bitch, and cunt," Molly had said with a bitter laugh. "They told me to shove my leaflets up my ass. So much for the tolerance of free speech."

Shamed by Molly's activism and her fervor, Dan went with her to a rally protesting the war in Chicago's Grant Park. But holding an antiwar sign in a mob of people, straining to hear the almost unintelligible voice of the Reverend Jesse Jackson carried hoarsely through the microphone, made him feel ridiculous. The young people around him seemed the age of his own students, and that left him detached from the protest and ill at ease. The signs around him not only condemned the prospects of war but often mocked and derided Bush, Cheney, and Secretary of Defense Donald Rumsfeld, exhibiting crude, sometimes obscene caricatures of the president and his staff. Dan had the disheartening feeling that many protesters were there simply to share in the excitement and not because of any strong principles against the war.

Yet the protests, warnings, and petitions proved futile against the administration's resolve. In March of 2003, bypassing the inability of the United States to gain an endorsement of its policies by the U.N. Security Council, President Bush launched Operation Iraqi Freedom. The initial stage of the war was marked by a devastating series of bombing raids called "Shock and Awe."

Each evening the television screen showed a panoply of explosions lighting the night sky in what seemed a massive Fourth of July celebration. But as they watched, Molly and Dan understood that those explosions meant innocent people were dying.

The Iraqi army seemed in total disarray, and the expected ferocity of the counterattack never materialized. In almost record time,
the resistance had crumbled and the terrible war had been won.
Rush Limbaugh on radio and Bill O'Reilly on television gloated
at the swiftness and ease of the war on the talk programs. They
mocked the "liberals" for their timidity and apprehension about
launching the "struggle against terrorism." In the first few weeks,
the TV networks played over and over again the scenes of the great
statue of Saddam being toppled.

In June of that year, two months after the outbreak of war in
Iraq, Noah graduated with scholastic and athletic honors from
Provincefield High School. The evening of his graduation, Dan
brought his father from the Veterans' Home, and, befitting a Medal
of Honor winner, the school administration placed Thomas Scott's
wheelchair in the front row of the auditorium. Dan and Molly sat
alongside him.

After Noah received his diploma to more thunderous applause
than that accorded any other student, he walked down the steps
from the stage and smiled at his family in the front row. Yet Dan
could not help noticing that his son's eyes lingered most lovingly and
with enormous pride on his grandfather. As he passed them, Noah
raised his fist in an exultant gesture over his head. And Thomas
Scott, his brawny, deteriorating frame swollen with pride and love
for this blood of his blood, raised his own great arm and, with his
gnarled fingers tightly clenched, pumped his fist fervently in the
air in response to the gesture of his grandson. It was, Dan thought,
with a pang of envy, as if grandson and grandfather were comrades
and the remainder of the family outsiders.

Noah worked that summer at the Kentucky Fried Chicken restaurant in Provincefield. Within two months he had been made
manager, and he carried the news proudly to his father, mother,
and grandfather when they were gathered at the house for Sunday
dinner.

"Why did those yahoos take two months to decide you were
manager material?" Thomas Scott said indignantly. "They should
have spotted that you had the right stuff sooner than that!"

"Give me some time, Gramps," Noah laughed. "It's a good start if I decide to work there next summer. I'll be making a lot more money."

"Give that boy a few years and he'd be managing a fleet of stores!" Thomas Scott said excitedly to Molly and Dan after Noah had left the room. "He's a winner!"

"He wants to go into astronomy, dad," Dan said.

"He can do whatever he wants to do!" Thomas Scott spoke emphatically. "Whether it's looking at the stars or running a major business. That boy's a winner!"

During his junior year in high school, Noah had applied to three colleges, and all three had accepted his applications. Two of them, including the University of Michigan, the school he decided to attend, promised him substantial scholarships.

That fall, Dan picked up his father at the Veterans' Home, and together they drove Noah to Ann Arbor for the beginning of his freshman year. Noah wheeled his grandfather through the corridors and into the dorm that would be his dwelling for the academic term.

"Reminds me of the barracks when I was in boot camp," Thomas Scott said. He gestured toward the row of beds. "One thing's for sure, boy; you won't get lonely."

After they'd eaten lunch together, Dan and his father prepared to leave. Dan wanted to hug his son but felt embarrassed in front of the other young men around them. He clasped Noah's shoulders and wished him well. But afterward, while bidding his grandfather farewell, Thomas Scott motioned Noah closer. Noah knelt and put his arms around his grandfather, resting his head on the old man's shoulder. The two remained in that position, not saying a word, for what seemed a long time. When Noah finally let him go, Thomas Scott shook his head brusquely.

"You'll be fine, boy," the burly old man said, his own voice husky with emotion. "You study hard and show these yahoos who you are. And remember, always do the honorable thing. You're a Scott, and don't forget it."

During Noah's freshman year at the university, the conflict in Iraq dragged on and the fighting intensified, the casualty count growing as a result of roadside bombs and suicide bombers. The conflict that President Bush once heralded as having its "mission accomplished" appeared to have no end in sight.

Noah appeared to Dan and Molly to grow restless. His grades fell from straight A's to include several B's and even a C, a grade he'd never received during his four years in high school. In response to Dan and Molly's concerned queries, Noah told them that he was having trouble settling down to study in the bustling, convivial environment of the populous university.

When he came home over the Christmas holidays, Noah seemed unusually somber and preoccupied. On several occasions, Dan had the feeling that his son was holding back something he wished to tell them.

A few days after New Year's, on an evening when several neighbors were over having cake and coffee, the conversation turned to Iraq. Molly repeated her persistent condemnations of the war and of the need for the U.S. military to disengage itself in Iraq. After their neighbors had left, Noah confronted his mother in the kitchen.

"Mike Connors, the black boy who lived in Crown Point and used to work at KFC with me, is in Iraq," Noah said quietly. "His family couldn't afford to send him to college. I think he and the others who are fighting there deserve our support."

"I don't have any problem with the boys fighting there, Noah," Molly said earnestly. "I just don't think we belong there. The war was launched for one reason that has proven unfounded and is now being waged for another equally invalid reason."

"I know that's what you believe, Mom," Noah said, his tone unusually sharp. "I'm just saying that every time you're around a few people, you don't have to get on your soapbox and deliver one of your tirades. Other people may have different feelings about the war and about the men and women fighting and dying there."

Before Molly had a chance to respond, Noah turned and left the kitchen.

"He's not thinking about whether the war is right or wrong," Dan said to reassure her. "He's seeing it in personal terms involving young men like Mike Connors."

Molly didn't answer but, with her movements quick and tense, turned back to loading the dishwasher.

The disabling, restless school year came to a climax when Noah returned home from Ann Arbor at the end of his freshman year in June of 2004 to tell Molly and Dan he'd enlisted in the Marine Corps. Molly was shaken and distraught and responded to the news with anger.

"You had no right to make such a decision on your own!" Molly cried. "You should have spoken to us first! You owe us that much!"

"I already knew where you stood, Mom," Noah shrugged. "All of Provincefield knows where you stand. I knew what you and Dad would say, so I made the decision for myself."

Dan was also heartsick at his son's enlistment in a war he and Molly thought reckless, but he feared protesting as fervently as his wife. There was a quiet resolve in Noah's manner that suggested he had already made up his mind. Dan didn't want his son to feel he wasn't being supported in whatever he decided to do. At nineteen, Noah was a fully grown man, two inches taller and much sturdier than Dan.

"There isn't any reason for you to give up your education now." Molly's anger had become pleading. "You've only completed your freshman year. Please, Noah, wait at least another year!"

"Other fellows are giving up their educations to fight," Noah said. "I'm not saying it's a war I believe is right. But whatever I think about it, our country is at war, and others are fighting for us. It's not fair that they should shoulder all the burden."

Molly looked imploringly at Dan.

"You know how your mom and I feel about this war," Dan said. "It's the wrong war at the wrong place at the wrong time."

"I don't want you to go," Molly said, her voice low and anguished.

Noah went to embrace his mother. Molly appeared small and vulnerable in their son's strong arms.

"Hey, Mom, lighten up," Noah said teasingly. "Every time I get into the car on a Friday night, something fatal can happen. Every time I board an airplane, something fatal can happen." He grinned and squeezed Molly. "Besides, you know I'm not reckless or foolhardy. I'm not trying to be a hero like Gramps. I just want to put in my share of service to my country."

Later, after Noah left the house to visit friends, Molly turned on Dan.

"He's doing this for your father," she said, her breathing tight and agitated. "He's doing it to make Thomas Scott feel proud of his grandson."

"That's not fair, Molly," Dan said. "Noah's a grown man, and he's made up his own mind. My dad would never urge him to go."

"You go talk to him!" Molly said, her voice trembling. "You go tell him to ask his grandson to stay in school! That's where Noah belongs now! Have him promise your father to remain at the university at least one more year. Perhaps by then this goddamn war will be over!"

"Molly, I don't think Dad will get him to change his mind."

"I'm asking you to ask your father to try!" Molly said, her voice low and hoarse. "Go to him now! Have him tell his grandson that all his tales of blood and war are an old man's dream of past glory! Tell him that if he feels any love for me at all, he'll talk to Noah now!"

With a burdened spirit, Dan left the house and drove to the Veterans' Home. He walked through the vestibule and down the hall to his father's room, which was empty. As he turned back into the hallway, a grizzled veteran named Willy Post he'd met on one of his visits came stumping along on his walker.

"Tracker's on the terrace," Willy Post said. "I saw him out there a few minutes ago."

Dan walked out onto the terrace and found his father alone in his wheelchair, staring out at the lawn and gardens. Thomas Scott wore a bulky turtleneck with a scarf around his throat; strands of his thick white hair were visible under his cap. His big slumped frame seemed too big for the chair.

The gardens and lawn stretching away from the terrace were in the first greening of summer, yellow tulips and scarlet hibiscus blooming among the winter's scrub. Above their heads, a few dense clouds hinted of rain.

When Dan came closer, his father looked up at him, his cheeks somber in the afternoon light.

"Hello, Dad."

"Hello, Danny," his father said. He gestured toward the trees.

"I been watching a gray squirrel trying to keep away from an angry blue jay that's following it from limb to limb. I figure she's trying to protect a nest of her fledglings somewhere in the trees."

He fell silent for a moment.

"I know why you're here," he said wearily. "Noah came to see me first." He paused, and looked up at Dan. His eyes were clouded and his voice troubled. "You and Molly may not believe me, but I tried to counsel him to wait. I told him there was plenty of time to join up. I figure this war is going to go on for a long time yet, and he'd have a chance to enlist later on. Honest to God, Danny, that's what I told him." His father looked down at his knees and rubbed the worn cloth of his trousers. A sigh of resignation passed his lips. "While I kept after him to wait, he looked at me like all the stories I been telling him for years were lies. He told me, you should have heard his voice, 'Gramps, I thought you'd be so proud.'" His father's voice trembled. "I was proud, I couldn't help feeling damn proud . . . but for Molly's sake, I couldn't tell him that. When I realized I'd disappointed him, I felt sick in my heart. I thought of you and Molly, and I tried to tell him not to go. But he wouldn't listen. He'd made up his mind." He looked at Dan, his strong face strangely insecure and helpless. "You think Molly will believe I tried?"

"I'll talk to her," Dan said, even as he understood that nothing he said would change Molly's mind. She had lived with the resentment of his father and his stories of war too long.

He sat down then on a bench beside his father's wheelchair. He was close enough to see his father's fingers trembling, his hand opening and then clenching again in his lap. They sat together in silence while in the garden a rabbit dashed across the open expanse of earth, leaving one haven to seek safety in another.

In that moment, Dan wished—a foolish, childish wish, he knew—that he had the power to freeze time, to stop the earth turning, to postpone the future.

Chapter 4

WHEN NEWS OF NOAH'S ENLISTMENT SWEPT THROUGH Provincefield, an outpouring of praise came from the townspeople. Although National Guard units had been called up in various regions of Indiana, there weren't any young men or young women from Provincefield in service. Noah Scott was the town's solitary contribution to the Iraq war.

The *Provincefield Gazette* ran a front page story that included a gladiatorial photograph of a fierce-eyed Noah after one of his high school football triumphs. The article stated, "It is fitting that our most celebrated military family, led by Thomas Joshua Scott, a Medal of Honor winner for valor in the Second World War, should now send another generation of warrior into the service of our country."

Noah returned from marine boot camp at the end of summer, looking martial and handsome in his uniform, his demeanor radiating confidence and resolve. In Provincefield, businesses and individuals made his homecoming a reason for celebration. The local Buick dealer offered an added 10 percent "Noah Scott discount" on any new Buick bought during that month. One of the well-frequented taverns in town, The Cave, advertised "Celebrate our Hometown Hero this coming Saturday night. First drink free in honor of Noah Scott."

While the older residents in town lauded Noah, the young men envied him, and a few spoke of following his example and enlisting. The prettiest girls in town vied for a chance to be seen with him. Emily Galvin, queen of the high school's Harvest Festival, a girl Noah had dated during his senior year, gave an interview to the town paper, saying that Noah was "the finest young man I'd ever dated."

At the high school, in the post office, and in the bank, people stopped Dan to congratulate him on his son following in the honorable tradition of the Scott family. The townspeople came to understand that the only member of the Scott family to whom they should avoid praising Noah's enlistment was his mother.

"I didn't want him to join the Marines!" she replied angrily to those who had the imprudence to congratulate her about Noah. "I think this war is a blunder! So don't tell me how proud I should feel!"

But her opposition was a slim reed in the whirlwind of flattery and adulation that surrounded the young serviceman. On the last Sunday of leave before Noah was to return to his base, the Scott family went to Sunday services at St. James Presbyterian Church.

When Noah pushed his grandfather's wheelchair into the church, the sight of the young marine in his resplendent blue and white dress uniform standing beside the aging hero of another war caused an excited murmuring to sweep the congregation. People twisted in the pews to steal glances at the grandfather with his grandson. In spite of the anxiety with which he had responded to his son's enlistment, Dan couldn't resist a feeling of pride at how his tall, handsome son riveted the attention of everyone in the church. Only Molly, somber and unsmiling, seemed to resist the excitement and the collective pride.

In his sermon that Sunday, Pastor Wiggam spoke of Noah's enlistment as a courageous and unselfish act.

"Some of us here, and I place myself among them, protested the war as being a flawed mission," Pastor Wiggam said gravely. "I know others feel it is a necessary conflict. But today, those who are for the war and those against the war can be united in our bond of admiration and affection for our own Noah Scott. His family has been a part of our community for years now, and I have watched this young man grow from childhood into sturdy manhood. Now, as with other young men and young women, he goes off in the service of his country. We wish him godspeed, and we will keep him in our prayers that he may return to us safely."

During the coffee hour that followed the end of the service, Noah stood beside his grandfather's wheelchair, the parishioners pressing in to speak to them and to shake their hands. The heroic aura that had always surrounded Thomas Scott seemed to gain a renewed luster in the presence of the young marine.

Dan stood in a corner beside Molly, and people did no more than nod and smile fleetingly at them as they passed. In those moments, witnessing Molly standing alone against the currents of praise, Dan admired his wife as a heroic figure in her own right.

That summer following Noah's enlistment, the bitter and divisive election campaign for the presidency, which had been in progress for almost a year, gained in animosity and fervor as November 6 came closer.

During the campaign, Molly and Dan, among a minority of Democrats in a town that was traditionally Republican, volunteered on behalf of Senator John Kerry. Both felt the contest to be one of the most tarnished presidential campaigns in their memory, with an abundance of slurs and defamations.

They watched the presidential debates between Bush and Kerry and, at one point, in response to a question from moderator Jim Lehrer to President Bush as to whether the Iraq experience would make him more reluctant to launch preemptive military operations in the future, the president insisted that he never wanted to commit troops but did so because "the enemy attacked us . . . and I have a solemn duty to protect the American people."

That brought a quick retort from Kerry.

"Saddam Hussein didn't attack us. Osama bin Laden attacked us. Al-Qaeda attacked us."

Molly jumped up, clapping her hands in jubilant agreement.

"That's right! That's the response! Shove his hypocrisy down his throat!"

In another debate, Bush defended his position to topple dictator Saddam Hussein, saying the sacrifice made by 1,059 U.S. troops who had been killed in Iraq was "noble and worthy" and would make the country safer in the long run.

"How can anyone believe that distortion of reality?" Molly cried. "The truth is that we're less safe as a nation today than we were before 9/11. Bush and his cronies have managed to make us the most hated country in the world!"

Dan looked with surprise at the impassioned involvement of his wife. He knew her to be a strong woman, but he could not remember her ever being quite as zealously partisan as she had become during the current campaign.

While Molly freely voiced her negative opinions of the president and his administration, Dan felt himself more constrained because of his position.

"Regardless of my own feelings," Dan said to Molly, "I've got to maintain some kind of neutrality. My students come from both Republican and Democratic homes."

"The Evangelicals and right-wingers don't worry about neutrality," Molly said. "Rush Limbaugh strives with the zeal of a fanatic to convince people his views are the gospel. And bellicose columnists like Krauthammer and Novak don't allow for the validity of any other opinion but their own!"

Molly's greatest objection to Kerry was his lack of opposition to the war.

"Getting us out of Iraq should be his first priority," Molly said. "He should make it an essential part of his platform to begin to bring our troops home as soon as he is elected. Set a timetable for our withdrawal, not only for our own sake but to spare the Iraqi people who are suffering those daily bombings."

There were people in Provincefield who condemned Molly, saying her virulent criticism of the war betrayed the troops, including her own son, serving in Iraq. Her response was that as the mother of a soldier, concerned for him as well as for the lives of other U.S. soldiers serving in Iraq, she had both a right and a responsibility to speak out against what she felt was an immoral and unjustified war.

Even Dan's students in a class discussion on the coming election became belligerent in rendering their opinions.

"The president doesn't deserve to be reelected because he lied about his service in the Texas National Guard!" Emily Rostow said.

"Kerry lied about his medals in Vietnam!" Kevin Kraft responded. "He came back and called all the U.S. soldiers who served there butchers."

"He never said that!" Rick Schroeder, one of Dan's brighter students said. "He showed courage in going to war, and once he'd seen what that war was like, he had the guts to return home and tell the American people it was a disaster!"

"You can't deny that he called our soldiers in Vietnam baby killers!"

"He was only telling the truth about massacres such as the one at My Lai when our soldiers slaughtered an entire village of Vietnamese men, women, and children!"

Dan tried to moderate the fervor of the discussions, seeking to prevent them from becoming overheated. But it was a stressful and tempestuous time, and passions ran high. At the VFW Post in Provincefield, during a public policy debate that Molly and Dan attended to air opposing views on the war, someone referred to the president as a "service-dodging cowboy," and a brawl erupted outside the post headquarters. Three Provincefield police cars had to be dispatched to restore order.

On election night, Dan and Molly watched the returns until after midnight. They switched channels from the reserved Jim Lehrer on public television, with his scholarly guests, to the major news anchors, Peter Jennings, Tom Brokaw, and Dan Rather. For a while, it appeared that Kerry was going to pull an upset, but then the tide turned against him. When the networks announced Bush as the winner, Molly rose wearily from the couch.

"We lived through Nixon and Agnew," Dan tried to console her. "We can survive four more years of Bush."

"I'm not so sure," Molly said, her voice heavy with resignation. "His administration wanted this war for reasons they haven't told the American people. Those hawks smell blood and are not going to pull our troops out of there now. God help us all."

The first letter they received from Noah at the beginning of September came from Kuwait. His impressions were those of a small-town youth experiencing an exotic, foreign land.

Dearest Mom, Dad, and Gramps:

Greetings from Kuwait!

We're assigned a couple of weeks of special training here before shipping out. I have to tell you that growing up in Provincefield doesn't prepare one for the incredible sights here. The mosques with their minarets, the chanting of the muezzin calling the faithful to prayers, and the tiny side streets with curtained cafés where old men sit smoking narghilas (water pipes) belong to the stories I once read about in the *Arabian Nights*. It is a fascinating world, but I expect it can be dangerous too. Our officers warn us about drinking and cursing in public and, above all, about respecting the women.

Now the truth is that you can't tell which of the girls or women here are pretty or even whether they're

eighteen or eighty because they all wear veils and
long dresses that cover them from neck to foot. I can
just imagine what the good citizens of Kuwait would
think if they saw the skimpy outfits our Cougar
cheerleaders wore (like the ones Mom used to wear!).

The other day I went on an excursion with a few
guys from our unit by bus to a valley full of the
most brilliant and colorful flowers. There were also
thousands of snow white birds unlike any I had ever
seen in my life. Truly, it was a stunning sight for a
small-town boy like me to witness. It made me think
of all the places in the world I'd like to visit someday.

I'm doing fine, so don't worry about me. All the
fellows in our outfit feel confident that we'll come
through this all right because we're well trained and
we have good officers.

Much love, Noah

"He sounds fine," Dan said after they'd finished reading Noah's
letter a second time. "He also sounds confident that they are as well
prepared as they can be with good equipment and good officers."

"How soon do you think they'll send them to Iraq?" Molly
asked.

"I suppose when their training is finished," Dan said. "They
won't send them before they feel the men are ready."

That evening, Dan stayed up later than Molly to grade papers.
Later, when he went upstairs to bed, he saw that she had fallen
asleep with Noah's letter still clasped in her hand.

That initial letter was followed a few weeks later by a second
letter, written after Noah's unit had deployed to Iraq.

Dearest Mom, Dad, and Gramps:

We have been in Iraq now for about two weeks,
and the destruction from the bombings and lack
of water and electricity are a real problem for the
Iraqis. The weather here is unbelievably hot. I think
of our summers back home when we have the air
conditioning going all the time and how much water

we used for the garden and Mom's hibiscus plants. That amount of water would keep a neighborhood here for a week.

We have been on a few patrols in our Humvees and, so far, things have been fairly quiet.

When we're not on patrol we stay in our compound, playing cards and telling stories. I have met a fellow Hoosier, Larry Dobson, who is a farm boy from Kouts, and we have become great friends. He is tall and lanky (kind of how Gary Cooper looked in *High Noon*) and has red hair and a wonderful sense of humor and he makes us laugh a lot. We are the only two Indiana boys in our unit and we have hit it off really well. We spend as much time together as we can.

I remember the times so many years ago when Dad and I read Homer's *Iliad* and how important a part of the story was the friendship of Achilles and Patroclus. I don't think Larry has read the *Iliad* or even heard of Homer, so I haven't said anything to him about it. If I think of him as Patroclus, I know that suggests I am thinking about myself as a warrior like Achilles, but that would be foolish. I'm just one marine among thousands stationed in a foreign land. The truth is that I wish the war here were like it was at Troy, men fighting in single combat with lances and swords.

Anyway, I better close now. I miss you all very much. Mom, don't worry about me. I am as safe as one can be. I'll write again as soon as I can.

Your loving son, Noah a.k.a. Achilles!

When Dan carried Noah's letter to the Veterans' Home to share with his father, Thomas Scott showed him a letter Noah had written solely to him.

Dear Gramps:

You'll get a lot of news in the letter I wrote to Mom and Dad so I won't repeat it here.

Things are much more dangerous than I wrote in the letter home. We are patrolling the road between Fallujah and Metrol where there have been a number of roadside bombings. We have already lost several of our men to suicide bombers. It is strange how your view of the world changes. There isn't any such thing as a safe area or an innocent object. Everything and everyone is dangerous. A car, a garbage can, a box. And you can never know who is a friend or an enemy. A soldier in the 32nd Brigade was killed when a child came up to take the bar of chocolate this poor grunt was offering. The kid, they say, couldn't have been more than thirteen or fourteen, and had a bomb strapped under his shirt that he detonated and blew them both up. I can't understand how they can send children on missions like that.

There's something else I don't understand. The hate. We can feel it when we're out on patrol, people watching us, not saying anything, just staring. The hate comes at us in waves. In a way it's unbelievable because, after all, we didn't invade Iraq to conquer them but to help them get rid of a dictator who brutalized them and had absolute power over their lives.

What are the best parts? The camaraderie, the huddling around to share stories, listening to Larry describe in vivid, erotic detail the girls he seduced and how he screwed them. Everyone suspects he's lying, but he tells the stories so dramatically we all love to listen. When we get home, we should try to get Larry on Leno or Letterman. He'd be a riot.

Anyway, Gramps, that's enough for now. Try to reassure Dad and especially Mom that things aren't really that dangerous here. I know how she feels about this war and how she worries.

Your loving grandson,
Noah

As Dan read the letter that starkly heightened his fear for his son, he could not help a feeling of envy because the letter Noah wrote to his grandfather was more honest about Noah's tour of duty in Iraq. And by addressing the letter only to his grandfather, Noah excluded Dan from that privileged fraternity of one soldier writing to another. His father sensed his distress.

"Don't feel bad, son," Thomas Scott said consolingly. "He would have sent this same letter to you at home except for his mother. He doesn't want to worry Molly. He knows that I'll share his letters with you."

In the weeks that followed, a strange game began for Dan: an adroit balancing between the letters Noah wrote to his mother (addressed to the three of them) and the letters he wrote to his grandfather at the Veterans' Home. The letters home were innocuous, filled with trivia about the Iraqi people and the efforts of the military to repair and rebuild electrical sites and water pumping stations. Noah assured his family that he lived with other marines in well-guarded compounds, that they ate well, and that his principal assignments were in less hostile regions of the city of Fallujah. He also enclosed several snapshots where he stood in a circle of grinning servicemen.

Molly read and reread the letters, poring over the pictures, displaying an anxiety that there were things Noah wasn't revealing to them.

"The papers and news programs are full of stories about suicide bombings and Iraqi civilians dying and insurgents attacking and killing our soldiers! Noah doesn't mention any of those things! He tells us so little he might almost be on duty at some base in the U.S."

"That's because he's in one of the safer areas," Dan said. "He can't make up danger if he's not in danger."

Molly shook her head in frustration.

"I have a gut feeling he's not telling us everything. He's trying to protect us."

She looked at Dan, and he felt the probing power of her eyes.

"Is he writing different letters to your father?"

Dan felt a tightness in his chest and a swirl of nausea in his stomach. He hoped his voice did not betray the lie.

"He sends dad some of the same snapshots and a few more lines about fellows in his outfit. You know, the kind of thing one soldier would write to another soldier."

That autumn, with Noah in Iraq and the relentless bombings continuing, a persistent anxiety shadowed Dan's days, a nagging unrest he carried into the beginning of the school year. He had a calendar on the wall in his office, and each morning he marked off another day. At the end of a week he was grateful because his son was one week closer to returning home.

He understood he was experiencing the apprehension every parent lived with who had a son or daughter away at war, emotions that made him assess life and his young students in darker shades.

The young boys and girls in his classes would have been surprised if he had shared his thoughts. He found himself staring at them with a greater intensity than he had ever been conscious of before, wondering how short or long the span of their lives would be. By the law of averages, several of them would be stricken by fatal illness or accident within a few years and not survive their youth. Some would live long, fulfilling lives and see the bounty of many children and grandchildren. Others would live solitary, lonely lives and die childless. Some would leave the small Indiana town and travel the world. Others would continue to live in Provincefield, marrying, working, and dying in the town where they had been born.

He felt a need to communicate these feelings to his students, telling them something of the ephemeral, precarious nature of life and how they should not take that life for granted. He knew these emotions were born out of fear for his son, but he couldn't help himself. He had become like an artist who could not look at a model without seeing the skull beneath the flesh.

Yet, he could not fashion the words to put that swirl of inchoate feelings into something coherent his students might understand. So he continued to intone the same lessons he had spoken so often, the words they expected to hear, and did not share with them those visions and emotions closest to his heart.

By the middle of October, the sequence of fall days still balmy with the lingering scents of trees and flowers, Dan's students seemed to have trouble concentrating. He saw them gazing out the open windows of the classroom, each boy or girl lost within his or her own thoughts.

There were times when his own attention wavered. He found himself staring pensively at a girl in his class who wore slacks and sandals, a small blonde ponytail cascading down her back. She reminded him of a girl Noah had dated in high school, a sweet, shy girl who had eaten dinner with them several times but whose name he couldn't remember. For a while Molly and he wondered if the two might become serious. Perhaps if Noah had a girlfriend he truly cared about, he would have shown less eagerness to enlist.

On another occasion, when a downy-winged robin alighted on the sill of their open classroom window, Dan thought of Noah's letter written about the white birds he had seen in Kuwait.

A voice broke into his reverie.

"Mr. Scott, I think you were daydreaming," Debbie Fairfield said with a teasing smile. "A penny for your thoughts."

The class laughed.

"I was just thinking how fortunate a teacher I am to have a class of such bright and perceptive students," Dan smiled.

Christmas that year seemed to Dan and Molly to be a spurious and hollow season. The decorative glitter of lights suspended around the houses along their block, the windows and lawns adorned with plastic Santas and artificial reindeer, all mocked their own melancholy.

They decided they'd put up a tree as they had always done when Noah was at home. Dan bought a smaller balsam than usual, and to help in the decoration, they invited over a few neighbors and their children. Dan planned to pick his father up from the Veterans' Home to join them, but his father begged off, saying he had a cold. That might have been true, but Dan had noticed that whenever his father was over for dinner, he displayed a certain uneasiness around Molly. His father knew that Molly blamed him for Noah's enlistment.

When their neighbors and the children arrived that evening to help with the tree, Dan carried down from the attic the box of lights and ornaments. While he unpacked the boxes, Molly served eggnog and cookies. For a little while the living room was filled with laughter and banter, and Dan was grateful to see Molly smiling several times.

After the neighbors had departed, Dan and Molly sat together on the couch. They had turned off the lamps, and the only illumination in the room came from the tree, the Christmas lights casting hues of various colors across the ceiling and walls.

"Do you think they'll have any kind of Christmas celebration for the soldiers?" Molly asked, her voice low and pensive. "The weather there is so hot, it must not seem like Christmas at all. They probably wouldn't have anything like a tree."

"They might have plastic trees," Dan said. "And I'm sure they'll have some kind of celebration. Probably eat a good Christmas dinner with turkey or prime rib and then maybe sing Christmas carols."

"I hope Noah received the box we sent him," Molly said.

"We mailed it early enough," Dan said. "Connie at the post office assured me it would get to Baghdad with time to spare."

They sat for a long time without moving or speaking, gazing at the tree. Molly lowered her head to rest against Dan's shoulder, her breast pressing against his arm so he could almost feel the slow and mournful throbbing of her heart.

Through January and February, Molly and Dan wrote letters regularly to Noah, Molly at least three times a week. She didn't show the letters to Dan, and he was at a loss to understand what she could find to write about. In his own letters, he soon exhausted what there was to tell his son about events in the town or in the school.

As the winter went on, Noah's letters home became shorter and more innocuous, letters Dan sensed were written out of a sense of obligation to reassure his parents rather than because he had anything to say. Even his handwriting became a hasty, careless scrawl.

> Dearest Mom, Dad, and Gramps:
>
> Not much news from here. We're spending a lot of time in our barracks since our presence on the roads seems to arouse the animosity of the Iraqis. We play cards and tell stories. It's hot but not as hot as it would be if we were patrolling in the sun. I know that

Provincefield is probably covered with snow and right
about now I wish I could be there to share it. As I've
written you before, don't worry about me. The time
is passing quickly and before you know it, my tour of
duty will be over and I'll be able to come home. Then
on Memorial Day, Gramps won't have to sit in the
reviewing stand alone. I'll be there beside him, maybe
even have a medal or two of my own. Don't get the
idea that I'm trying for any medals. I'm just trying to
do my duty and get through my days.

I love you all very much,
your son and grandson, Noah

When Dan drove to the Veterans' Home on a day in late March,
a letter Noah had written to his grandfather was stark and grim.

Dear Gramps:

My friend Larry Dobson was killed yesterday. He
was on patrol in a Humvee when a roadside bomb
went off underneath it. He and three other marines
were killed. I still can't believe it. He had such vitality
and life in him. I know it's hard to believe, since I've
known Larry only a few months, but I feel as I would
feel if you or Dad or Mom died.

For the first time since coming here I feel myself
filled with anger and a desire for vengeance. I want
to take my M-16 and find a crowd of goddamn Iraqis
and blast them to hell and gone. But that doesn't
make much sense. Who would I kill? Some poor
sonofabitch in ragged clothes trying to scavenge bread
for his family?

I got to stop now. Nothing makes sense, even these
words I'm putting down. I'm sick of this country
and having to watch the people we're here to save,
especially the children, suffering. Some of our medics
treat them when they can, but there isn't much that
can be done. They don't have the medications or
the food and clean water they need. I'm also sick of

the weather, which is relentlessly hot. In addition to
the heat, a week ago there was a sandstorm unlike
anything I ever experienced before. For days nothing
moved, and we remained huddled in our barracks.
After the storm we had sand in the engines of our
tanks and trucks, sand in our backpacks and pallets,
even sand in our food so everything tasted gritty and
shitty.

I'm sorry, Gramps, but maybe I'm not the soldier
I should be, the kind who takes whatever comes
without complaint, the kind of soldier you were. But
this isn't like any war you ever told me about. Our
enemy is invisible, and the only way we know he's
been there is when the damn roadside bombs go off.
When we go out on patrol to hunt the bastards, I get
the uneasy feeling that we are the ones being hunted.

Gramps, you must think me a poor example of a
stalwart Scott warrior, but the honest, damn truth
is that I don't feel much like a courageous warrior.
Maybe that's because our enemy here is heat, sand,
hidden bombs, and the suffering of people around
us. There's something wrong here, but I'm not smart
enough to figure out what that is.

Your loving grandson, Noah

Dan read and reread the letter several times, feeling a knot in
his stomach, a trembling in his knees.

"That's a hard thing for any soldier," his father said, grief and
concern for his grandson etched sharply into his cheeks. "Losing
a comrade, a man you've eaten with and fought with, a man who
has slept beside you. It's like losing a brother. A man never really
gets over such a loss." His father paused. "How is Molly doing?"

"She's finding Noah's letters harder and harder to believe."

"She's too smart a gal to be fooled. She knows better. She's a
strong woman, too, and maybe she deserves to be told the truth."

"If she were to read the letters Noah sends to you, she'd be sick
with worry," Dan said. "Besides, if we showed her his letters now,
she'd know that we've been deceiving her for months."

They sat without speaking for a while, his father holding Noah's letter limply in his hand, staring out the window of his room.

"I should have tried harder to persuade the boy not to go." His father's voice was low and troubled. Dan saw his somber face reflected in the glass of the window.

"He'd already enlisted when he came home from Ann Arbor," Dan said. "I don't think you or anyone else could have changed his mind."

"Maybe I shouldn't have told him all those stories . . ." his father's forlorn voice trailed weakly away.

They sat in silence for a few minutes longer.

"I guess I'll be leaving, Dad," Dan said.

"Good-bye, son." His father did not turn from the window. "Give Molly my love."

Chapter 5

THAT WINTER, MARCH WAS COLD AND APRIL CAME IN even colder. North of Provincefield, the lake remained frozen, its shoreline bearing twisted ice sculptures fashioned by storms. Not until the beginning of May did the final mounds of snow and ice melt, and spring buds appeared in the winter gardens and on the barren trees.

Through those months of snow and cold, Molly and Dan passed the routine of their days as they had been doing for years: he taught his students at the high school and Molly worked with the stroke patients at the Heart Center. In the evenings they ate dinner at home, resisting the TV news programs with the grim recitals of the civilian and military casualties in Iraq. Dan told Molly stories about students in his classes, and Molly related experiences with patients with whom she worked. They tried to avoid speaking constantly about Noah, although they understood their son was on both their minds.

Molly continued vigorously opposing the war, writing letters to members of the Congress and the Senate about setting a withdrawal date to bring the troops home. She also corresponded with peace groups across the country and made plans to join a peace rally these groups planned in Washington for the fall.

Molly also spent time in the evening on her computer, surfing the Web sites where mothers of young men and young women serving in Iraq made contact with one another. There were mothers opposed to the war as Molly was and also mothers who supported the military service of their sons and daughters and who felt the war was justified.

From time to time, Molly printed out letters and read them to Dan.

"I find it hard to believe there are mothers who take pride in their son's death," she said. "This Ohio mother writes, 'While I grieve for my son's death, it makes me proud to know he died in the service of our country.'" She paused to look somberly at Dan. "Perhaps that's the kind of stoic woman you should have married."

"I married you because I loved you," Dan said.

"And I married the man I loved," Molly said softly. She held up another letter. "This one is from a mother who joined other families who had lost sons or daughters and met with President Bush. She writes that as the president tried to express his condolences, his voice choked up. He kept saying to the families, 'I am sorry, I'm so sorry.'"

"He wouldn't be human if he didn't feel their grief," Dan said.

"I don't doubt that he truly wants to console them," Molly said. "But it would be an even greater consolation to so many other families if he admitted the war was a colossal blunder and promised to bring our troops home."

In the first years following their marriage, Molly and Dan had made love frequently. Filled with desire for his lovely bride, Dan was easily aroused by the ripple of Molly's thighs under a light frock, by the way her lips glistened after she'd sipped from a glass of wine, by a teasing, wanton glance she cast at him when they were with other people, a glance that excluded everyone but the two of them. Those flirtations and incitements would conclude with their ardent lovemaking.

As they grew older, they continued to make love from time to time. But the passing years and the weariness both felt after a long day's work made their lovemaking less frequent.

Molly's worry about Noah in Iraq had her feeling anxious and depressed, and she and Dan hadn't made love in several months.

But on a night during that bleak, unsettled winter, they began their lovemaking once again.

Earlier that day they had received another brief, terse letter from Noah, repeating the same reassurances he had offered in previous letters. He was well and spending most of his time in the barracks, which contained a Ping-Pong table and a small gym with stationary bikes. In the free time they were allowed, he was playing Ping-Pong and exercising to keep himself fit. He thanked them for sending along the soap and shampoo and promised he'd write again soon.

With each of Noah's letters, Molly became more convinced that he was concealing the truth from them about the conditions in Iraq.

"I know he's trying to protect us," Molly said to Dan, her voice tense and distressed. "The news is full of the bloodshed in Iraq, bombings and people dying, and he wants us to believe he's spending his time playing Ping-Pong!"

At night, Molly had been having trouble sleeping, and their family doctor had prescribed sedatives for her. Sleep still remained elusive, and her restlessness worried Dan and affected his own sleep. But that night in March, a wind shaking the panes of their bedroom windows and the eaves of their house, Molly shifted closer to Dan in the bed. She reached out to touch him in a soft, erotic caress. When he took her into his arms, she kissed him ardently, the softness of her breasts pressing against his chest.

His own desire sparked, he felt the silkiness of her nightgown under his fingers. As he took her into his arms, he breathed the familiar scent of her, the aromatic talcum she used and the sweet smell of her hair. He slipped his hand beneath the gown and fondled the mounds of her breasts, ran his fingers down the firmness of her belly, caressed the smoothness of her thighs. After the months of abstinence, it seemed to him that her body was whiter than he remembered, her breasts the whitest of all. They made love then with a passion they hadn't experienced in many months.

Afterward, lying beside his wife in bed, her cheek resting against his shoulder, he felt her pulse grow slower and more tranquil. Despite his gratefulness at the intimacy of love fulfilled, he understood that Molly's urge to make love was driven less by desire for him than by a need to deaden for a little while her anxiety about Noah. It was, he thought pensively, love without the joy and laughter he remembered sharing with her in the past.

There was a day in the middle of May, a day that began like many others that spring. Dan remained at school later than usual counseling a student who was failing one of his courses. On his drive home, his car windows open, the first scents of spring filled him with an unusual buoyancy. He was also heartened because, in Noah's most recent letter, their son had written that after he'd completed a year of duty, he'd be eligible for a furlough. While such a visit was still several months away, the prospect of having Noah with them even for a short time cheered both Molly and Dan.

He arrived home as daylight receded into twilight, the lawns and houses along the street taking on softer hues. Moths fluttered about the glowing gas lamp on their lawn, and the trilling of cicadas rose from the cluster of bushes beside the porch.

Molly's car was parked on the street in front of the house, but the kitchen, where she would have been preparing dinner, was dark. The adjoining rooms were also shadowed and silent. He thought it unlikely she'd be visiting a neighbor's house during the supper hour.

He called her name. When there wasn't any answer, he walked upstairs and looked in the bedrooms. He called her name once more and started down the stairs, an uneasiness stirring in his chest.

He entered the dark kitchen and flipped the switch on the wall. When the overhead neon lights flashed on, he uttered a startled cry. Molly was sitting at the kitchen table.

"Didn't you hear me, hon? I called your name four, five times! Why are you here in the dark?"

She looked at him in silence, her eyes strangely pale in the chalky circles of her face. He felt the pressure in his chest knotting harder.

"Molly! What is it?"

She kept staring at him mutely.

"Molly, for God's sake, say something!" he pleaded. "Are you sick?"

When she finally spoke, her voice was low and strangely toneless.

"After I got home, a car drove up to the house." She paused. "I think it was a Taurus."

Her voice trailed away, and he waited tensely for her to go on.

"Two men got out," she said. "They were tall, handsome men with the buttons on their dress uniforms shiny and polished in the sunlight."

He felt a stab of terror, a sudden urge to flee the house and escape her voice.

"I didn't answer the door," she said, "but they wouldn't leave. They knew I was inside, that I was hiding, and they kept ringing and knocking, knocking and ringing. They weren't going away, and when I finally answered, two marines who had driven up in a Taurus stood there. They looked like twins."

He felt his heart flailing in his chest. The room reeled, and he grasped at a chair to keep himself from falling. He wasn't sure he heard the words she spoke telling him their son was dead.

"For God's sake, Molly!" his voice echoed like a drumbeat in his ears. "They make mistakes! It must be a mistake!"

"They were so courteous," she continued in the same flat, almost impassive voice, "kind and caring as professional emissaries carrying news of death should be. I was trying not to scream and I started talking about Noah, telling them what a fine young man he was. They listened politely to everything I was saying and I didn't want them to leave. . . I didn't want to be left alone . . . so I told them about the Scott legacy, about Noah's grandfather winning the Medal of Honor and all the other Scott heroes. I told them how proud Noah's grandfather would be."

He thought grief had driven her mad.

"Molly, he'll be devastated! You know how much he loves Noah! He'd give his life for him!"

She didn't seem to hear him.

"I told them how proud your father would be," she went on. "How elated he'd feel because the Scott warrior legacy was unbroken. His grandson, Noah, sacrificing his life in the line of duty."

"Molly, for God's sake, Molly . . ."

"Oh, he will grieve," she said, a crooked parody of a smile creasing her cheeks, "but in the end, his pride will vanquish his grief. All that will matter is that every war this country has fought has been honored with Scott blood. Your father will cry for Noah, but his warrior heart will burst with pride."

"Molly!" he begged, his plea frail against her merciless voice. "You're not talking sense! Molly, in God's name . . . that's unfair!"

"On Memorial Day he'll be able to sit even more proudly in the reviewing stand. His father fought at the Marne, his uncle Paul in Korea, his cousin Douglas in Vietnam. Now his grandson has been added to that noble ledger of Scotts who served and died."

Suddenly, the immensity of what had happened to them overwhelmed him. Their son, Noah, was dead. All the months of anxiety and terror they had endured were justified, as if they had known from the beginning, the very beginning, that their son would not return alive.

Yet, in that shattered moment, Molly's rage and bitterness overwhelmed even their son's death. He started toward her, but, her eyes blazing, she waved him away.

"Don't come near me!" she cried, her voice cutting at his flesh like a knife. "Just go to your father now! Go tell him his grandson has been added to the Scott legacy of honor!"

"Molly, you're talking crazy!" He felt his body trembling, a fierce pain searing his chest. "He'll be heartbroken! In God's name, it isn't his fault! It's crazy to blame him!"

"You go now and tell the bloodthirsty old warrior the good news!" she cried, an eruption of fury distorting her face, making it appear swollen and ugly. "Tell him that for as long as I live, I'll pray he burns in hell for what he's done to my son!"

Helpless to withstand her frenzy and rage, he turned and fled from the house.

He drove aimlessly through the quiet streets of the town, turning corners at random, stopping for a red light, not moving when the light turned green until a horn blared behind him. He drove past the town's Memorial Park, with the platform where the high school band played during the Memorial Day and Fourth of July celebrations. Surrounding the bandstand, the spruce and pine trees, which had been decorated for Christmas, were now bare, the branches stark and gaunt under the beams of the street lamps.

He waited at a railroad crossing before the flashing red lights and watched the train passing in a blur of cars and a roar of wheels.

The sound of the train subsided, and when the gates rose, he drove across the tracks.

At the eastern edge of town, the signs above the fast food restaurants illuminated the night sky. He drove by McDonald's and Burger King and the Kentucky Fried Chicken where Noah had worked during his summers.

After he left Provincefield, the highway ran between empty stretches of landscape broken only by farmhouses and the looming structures of barns and silos. There were small, lighted windows visible in the farms, and he imagined people eating their dinners, unaware of the calamity that had struck his house.

His son's death was agony enough to bear. Yet Molly's bitterness and rage made their loss something even more unbearable. He was terrified for her and, at the same time, stricken with despair at having to tell his father about Noah's death. As the miles of dark highway rolled by, Dan cried; the tears blurred his eyes, and the road before his headlights appeared smeared and obscured. For a moment he embraced the thought that he might crash and die.

He realized, finally, that he was driving in the wrong direction, and at the next light he made a U-turn and started back the other way. For a moment he considered waiting until the next day, favoring daylight over darkness as a time to break the news to his father. But he dreaded having to return home to confront Molly, attempting to reason with her, trying to calm her rage.

He parked in the lot outside the Veterans' Home. For a long time he remained unmoving in the car, the engine idling, his hands grasping and twisting the wheel. His tears had dried and felt cold on his cheeks. His dread at having to tell his father about Noah passed into resignation. He left the car and walked slowly toward the building.

"Good evening, Mr. Scott," Susan, the receptionist, said.

"Good evening," he said.

"I saw your father a little while ago in the lounge playing checkers with Mr. Grafton."

Dan walked toward the lounge. Barbara Perkins, small and trim in her white nurse's uniform, greeted him. He usually paused to chat with her, but at that moment he didn't dare stop or he would have blurted out the news about his son.

In the lounge, several veterans were watching a ball game on the large television set. Len Grafton, who had been wounded and decorated in the Battle of the Bulge, sat on one of the couches holding a newspaper. Another veteran dozed in an armchair. His father wasn't in the lounge.

Grafton spotted Dan and called to him across the room.

"Your father's back in his room, Danny," he said with a broad grin. "I beat him at checkers and he's sulking."

For a moment Dan lingered in the doorway of the lounge, staring at the old men whose aging hearts still pulsed and kept them alive. Noah's strong young heart should have allowed him to live at least as long as the oldest of them had lived. A line he had read came back to him: "Better to be last among the living than first among the dead."

Walking the corridor to his father's room, he felt a pressure in his bladder and stopped in a rest room. As he washed his hands, he stared at his reflection in the mirror, expecting to see the ravages of grief etched in his face. But he saw only the same bland and irresolute countenance that he had lived with for a lifetime, his cheeks pale and his eyes watery.

When he reached his father's room, the door was closed. He knocked and then entered.

His father was just coming out of the bathroom, his wheelchair propped in the doorway. He braced himself against the wall with one hand while with the other he fumbled with the zipper on his pants. He looked dejected and tired, an old man who had finished pissing, wary he might fall, trying to zip up his pants.

"What you doing here this late, Danny?" his father asked. "You're lucky you didn't come earlier, in time for dinner. They had those damn salmon patties. I know how you feel about salmon patties."

His father halted his effort at zipping up his pants and then, still holding to the wall, reached the bed and sat on the edge. Dan noticed a button missing on his sweater. In the past, Dan would have taken the sweater to Molly, who would have sewn the button on and washed the garment as well. Now he wasn't sure what he would do.

"How you feeling?" he asked, the words a line from an old refrain he had spoken countless times.

"I still got trouble with my feet swelling," his father said. "That Indian doctor who comes here on Mondays thinks it's poor circulation in my legs." He paused. "Did you come because you thought I had a letter from Noah? I haven't heard from the boy now for almost two weeks, not since the last letter you read."

Dan stood there, trying to muster the courage to speak. His mouth felt parched, his heart torn with anguish for himself and with pity for the old man on the edge of the bed.

"What is it, Danny?" His father's usually strong voice faltered. "You and Molly having some trouble? Is that why you come by?"

Still he couldn't speak. His father stared at him uneasily.

"I was getting ready for bed," he said, and he reached nervously across the spread to smooth his pillow. "You don't usually come by this late. Maybe you better leave now and let me get some rest. The doc said I should keep my feet elevated much as I can."

He fell silent and looked back at Dan. His cheeks trembled as if the bone beneath the flesh had loosened.

"It's Noah," his father said finally, and, as if he were having trouble breathing, the words came out in a low, hoarse voice. "I been afraid of something like this happening. The boy's been wounded. All the damn bombings and shootings in that goddamn country." He paused, his face ashen, his eyes pleading. "That's it, isn't it, Danny? Noah's been wounded? That's what you come to tell me?"

"Noah's dead," Dan said. The words burned his lips. He watched his father at that moment and thought suddenly of a cartoon, an animation where the figure suddenly dissolves, flesh and bone turning molten, trickling down.

His father raised one hand, clenched into a fist, and waved it furiously at Dan.

"Goddamn it, no!" he cried, his voice harsh with outrage. "That's a goddamn lie! They're always getting those casualty lists and names mixed up! Noah's all right! You hear me? Don't you think I'd have felt it in my gut if anything were wrong?" He shook his head vehemently. "Goddamn it, I tell you Noah's all right! The boy's all right!"

The words tumbled in a storm from his father's lips. Then he reached down and began tugging at the zipper once more, trying furiously to close his fly. Finally, he stopped fumbling and looked up at Dan.

"Jesus Christ," he said and the words came in a stricken moan from his lips. "Jesus Christ . . . oh Jesus Christ . . . Jesus Christ . . . !"

In that moment, it was as if the valorous, strong face his father had worn for years had been a mask that was suddenly stripped away. Dan saw him for what he was, a weary, dying old nursing home king, shattered as Priam must have been shattered by the death of his son, as fathers and grandfathers had grieved who had lost sons at Shiloh and Chickamauga and Omaha Beach and Tet and Pyongyang and, now, Iraq.

By the time Dan returned home and drove his car into the garage, it was nearly five in the morning. He was exhausted and drained of tears. The nurse at the Veterans' Home had given Thomas Scott a sedative, and Dan sat beside his bed for several hours, watching his father's agony battling the effects of the medication. Finally, exhausted and inconsolable, his father succumbed to a drugged sleep that shielded him for a while from his pain. Dan told the nurse he'd return first thing in the morning.

He entered the house quietly, the rooms around him dark and silent. He listened for any sound to indicate whether Molly might still be up. He walked up the stairs, into the hallway, thinking about making up his bed in another room. But he needed to be close to Molly, whether or not she wanted him beside her.

He stripped to his underwear in the bathroom and then washed, his hands trembling. From the bathroom he walked barefooted into the shadowed bedroom.

The partial moon he'd seen over the highway had given way to the glimmerings of dawn, which cast a faint light through the curtains of the bedroom windows, illuminating the dresser, chair, and headboard of the bed. He saw the shape of Molly's figure under the blanket but couldn't tell whether she was asleep.

Dan followed a trail of light to his side of the bed and carefully pulled down the quilt. He slipped quietly between the sheets. Fearing a resurgence of her rage, he held himself warily near the edge of the mattress. He felt his heart throbbing, and he braced himself for her angry rejection.

He lay still for several minutes, listening for Molly's breathing. Then she turned in the bed, a slow shifting of her body toward him. Her hand touched his arm, her fingers coming to rest against his flesh in a gesture of acceptance. He was overwhelmed with gratefulness. He reached out and took Molly's hand and felt the softness of her fingers, which he gently kissed. He moved closer, their bodies touching, leg against leg, foot against foot. He felt the coldness of her flesh.

They lay together in silence while outside their house the dawn gained dominance over moonlight, objects in the room growing lighter. Somewhere in the distance, Dan heard the plaintive whistle of a train.

Molly spoke for the first time, her voice weary and resigned, drained of the rage and bitterness.

"What will we do?" Her words hung mournfully in the stillness. "How will we live?"

He had no answer except to hold her tightly.

"I've always known," she said. "From the beginning . . . when I first learned we would have a son, I knew. I knew that the day would come, sometime, somewhere, he'd be old enough for a war . . ."

"I should have pressed him harder about his enlistment," Dan said remorsefully. "I should have made it clear to him that we didn't want him to go. He should have asked us before he enlisted."

"It wouldn't have made any difference," Molly said quietly. "From the moment he was born, the history of this family decreed Noah would be a soldier. Nothing would have changed that."

As daylight lightened the shadows, he felt her moving slightly, a slight rocking motion of her body against his arm, which he understood as a ritual of grief.

In that sorrowful moment, he had a haunting recollection of Molly's beauty as a bride, her dark hair adorned in a sheer lace veil, her slender figure clad in a shimmering white gown. He remembered how endearing her lovely face appeared with a smudge of wedding cake on her cheek. He struggled suddenly to recall if there was anything in that jubilant, carefree celebration to intimate that one day they'd endure such heartbreak.

He considered the emptiness of life ahead of them now. They'd rise to go to work, eat, and sleep, following the same routine of hours, days, and nights they had lived for years. Yet, everything would be different because their son was no longer alive. Molly was right. How would they live? What would they do?

"How was your father?" she asked.

"The nurse sedated him," Dan said. "I sat with him until he fell asleep." For a few moments she was silent again.

"It isn't only my pain and my loss," she said. "I know your father's pain and the pain you feel. I know you both love him as I love him." Her sad, forlorn voice echoed from the hidden corners of the room. "Yet, no man can truly experience a mother's grief. A man makes a baby and walks away. But the woman retains the seed and nurtures it for all those months, feeling the fetus growing in her body, feeding on the food she eats, absorbing the liquid she drinks, breathing the air she breathes." She paused to draw breath, and he felt her trembling. "And then, a day comes when that baby emerges from her womb, the cord cut, to begin a life of its own. But the bond that comes of those months the two lived in one body is never really severed. When the child dies, something in the woman dies as well." She paused. "If men felt the death of a child as a woman feels it, they would no longer tolerate or condone any war."

Yes, he thought when she finished, yes. He had lived almost half a century and he hadn't until that moment understood the simple and profound truth she spoke.

Chapter 6

IF THEY HAD LIVED IN THE ENVIRONS OF A LARGE CITY, their sorrow and loss might have been observed and shared only by family and a few friends. But with the news of Noah's death, all of Provincefield went into mourning. In the days that followed, every morning Dan and Molly found fresh flowers and cards of condolence outside the door of their house. All the flags in town flew at half mast. Wherever they went, into the post office, grocery, hardware store, library, people spoke to them, expressing their grief, making efforts to console them. Friends they met on the street embraced them, their eyes moist with tears. Whether people thought the war justified or unjustified did not matter. The sympathy the two received on all sides was genuine and heartfelt.

Faced with this outpouring of compassion and sympathy, Molly, Dan, and Thomas Scott were constrained about allowing their own grief to diminish the aura of public mourning around Noah's death. Through those days, each of them fashioned a posture and behavior to fit what was expected of the family of a fallen soldier. Thomas Scott retreated into a demeanor of rigid control, accepting the condolences quietly and with a grave composure. Molly, bitter about the war she thought senseless, curbed her outrage, finding sanctuary in a resigned silence. Only Dan understood the terrible dimension of her despair because she felt their son had died in a useless and unnecessary war.

As for himself, not wishing to reveal any less composure than his wife and his father, he struggled to keep his grief to himself. He cried often, calling out his son's name, but only when he was alone and when no one could see or hear him.

A week after they received news of Noah's death, their son's coffin was flown in by transport to O'Hare Field in Chicago. A group of veterans from the VFW Post in Provincefield escorted the coffin in a black hearse to the Indiana state line. At that point, Indiana state police cars joined the procession and accompanied it to Provincefield, where police from communities across the county formed an honor guard escorting the hearse slowly through the town whose residents lined the street in tearful silence.

A memorial ceremony was held in the Provincefield High School football stadium attended by the townspeople as well as several thousand other residents from across Porter County. The large signpost on the football field used to display the scores of games played by the Cougars bore in large letters the message FOR OUR CLASSMATE, CPL. NOAH THOMAS SCOTT, IN LOVING MEMORY, IRAQ 5/12/05.

Noah's funeral was held in St. James Presbyterian Church in Provincefield on a balmy spring day in the middle of May, the air warm with the scent of newly budding flowers. Almost the entire population of the town as well as citizens from surrounding towns jammed the church and overflowed into the streets. The *Indianapolis Star* sent a correspondent to report on the funeral, and local news stations covered the ceremony as well. On the steps of the church, reporters interviewed students and teachers who had known Noah, shared his classes, and played various sports with him.

Inside the church, a squad of marines in dress uniform formed an honor guard, standing at rigid attention around Noah's coffin. One of them, handsome and white-gloved, bowed and presented Dan and Molly with their son's Purple Heart. Then the marine turned and snapped to attention before Thomas Scott, briskly saluting the old soldier, who sat in the front row of the church in his wheelchair.

As he delivered the eulogy, Pastor Wiggam spoke of watching Noah grow up and seeing him in church on Sundays. He also expressed the pleasure he felt in watching him play so superbly for the Cougars as well as in the grace and warmth Noah displayed in his relationship with others.

"If there are those here today," Pastor Wiggam said, "who would ask me to explain why the Lord would take from us a young man as magnificent as Noah Scott, I would find it hard to answer." He paused, staring somberly across the crowded, silent church. "I have been a pastor now for almost thirty-five years, and I retain my faith in God's wisdom beyond our understanding. Does my faith at times waver? I admit to you now that it does. But then neither is God infallible. Pause for a moment and consider that even God does not have the power to undo the past.

"So I confess to you now that in the dark night of the soul, I have moments when I weep as I pray, when I ask the Lord, why? Why should children die? Why should the innocent suffer? Why does he not show me his face to quell my doubt and ease my heart?"

Somewhere inside the church an infant's cry broke out, its shrill, plaintive wail shattering the stillness. After a moment, the cry ended as abruptly as it had begun.

"I have no easy answer for any of you or for myself," Pastor Wiggam said, "no reassurance to offer except to tell you that through the years I have come to believe that those who claim faith in God but without passion in the heart, without anguish of mind, without uncertainty and, yes, even at times without despair, believe only in some waxwork effigy of God and not in God himself."

His gaze swept across the church, and Dan felt the anguish in the man's spirit.

"I endure such a moment of despair now," Pastor Wiggam said. "In this moment, I ask why, why . . . why should this superb young man be dead, and why should I still live? Why? . . . Why? . . ."

His voice suddenly broke, and Dan saw him struggling to maintain his composure. Then the pastor's efforts collapsed, and he lowered his head and raised his hands weakly to his temples. By the way his shoulders and body trembled, Dan knew he had broken down into tears.

Several days after the funeral, in a letter they received from Noah's commanding officer, Molly and Dan learned the details of their son's death.

> Noah's unit was on patrol in a place called Karabilah when we received word that insurgents had ambushed a marine convoy. The men drove to the location in their Humvees. They stopped several cars not far from where the ambush had taken place. While they were questioning the car's occupants, guarding the men with their M-16 rifles, one of the suspects drew a grenade from under his coat and pulled the pin. Noah threw himself on the man and the grenade, smothering them with his body, to protect his fellow marines. The full force of the grenade cost him his life, but his action unquestionably saved a number of his comrades from death or serious injuries. For his valorous action, conduct performed in the noblest tradition of the Corps, I am today writing the Marine Corps Headquarters in Washington, strongly recommending your son for the Medal of Honor.

In the days that followed the funeral, the town commissioned a large black granite headstone to be placed on Noah's grave in the Provincefield cemetery. The inscription on the stone read "NOAH THOMAS SCOTT, 1984–2005, BELOVED BY ALL WHO KNEW HIM." Throughout the following weeks, Molly or Dan visited the grave every day, alone or together, to polish the granite and lay a flower on the mound of freshly turned earth.

As summer went on, the yellow ribbons faded on the trees. The flowers and cards placed before their house grew fewer and then ceased as the residents of Provincefield turned again to the daily business of living. Dan understood that the surge of life was inevitable, those still living not able to linger for long on the passing of individuals. Meanwhile, the war in Iraq went on, the controversy about its validity and the toll of its wounded and dead continuing as well.

Dan still received letters and e-mails filled with praise for his son. An anonymous donor from Indianapolis set up a $25,000 scholarship, named the Noah Thomas Scott Scholarship, to be given annually to an outstanding Indiana high school student.

On the Fourth of July, the town dedicated the holiday to Noah. The governor of Indiana issued a proclamation designating it Noah Scott Day. Their U.S. congressman came and spoke of Noah's valor and how proud his town, his state, and his country were of his contribution.

For Molly, Dan, and Thomas Scott, their grief did not lessen but receded deeper into the flesh and bone of their bodies. There were days Dan even saw Molly smile and, once or twice, heard her laugh. But it was a different laughter from what it had been in the past. A strangeness had entered their lives.

He understood the pain of loss that Molly and his father felt. Yet, to witness others' suffering was to recognize the barrier that separated human beings. Each man and woman had to suffer alone.

After her initial rage against Thomas Scott on the day she learned of her son's death, Molly never voiced any accusation against or condemnation of him again. Whatever her feelings, she remained cordial to Dan's father, inviting him for dinners in their house as she had done in the past. She washed his clothing that Dan carried back clean to the Veterans' Home.

Despite Molly's forbearance, Dan knew that his father understood Molly felt he bore the blame and responsibility for Noah's death. There were times Dan caught his father silently watching her, his face reflecting anguish and remorse. As for Dan's own mourning, he often thought of his son, grieving that he'd lost the hope of every father that he die before his son.

He also foresaw with a pervasive clairvoyance the course each of their lives would take. Molly would continue to fight against the war, hoping to save other sons and to spare other mothers. She'd look after her patients with that same compassion and devotion she had shown them in the past. In her last moments on earth, Dan believed that her final thoughts would be of the son she had lost.

His father would also mourn Noah in those few years he still had to live His pride as an old soldier would keep him composed in the presence of others. Dan could not know whether his father's final thoughts would be of heroic glory won in battle or of the death of his grandson.

Dan would go on living, as well, his own wound never healing. He'd see fragments of Noah reflected in the faces and voices of students he taught. Perhaps he'd realize some consolation by helping other young people understand the fleeting and precious essence of their days.

Near the end of summer, Dan sat playing checkers with his father in the garden of the Veterans' Home. A number of old men were in the garden as well, some sitting on the benches, others in their wheelchairs, scarred old roosters soaking up the warmth of the weakening sun. Among the trees in the garden, the maples and catalpas were beginning to display the first brown and scarlet leaves.

As if he'd forgotten the game, his father leaned back in his wheelchair, staring in silence at the changing foliage on the trees.

"You know, I never thought much about God," he said pensively. "I mean, when you consider what I've seen, it's hard to believe that he wouldn't abandon us all for what we do to one another." He paused. "Now, you know, Danny, I've begun to pray again. Every night and every morning, I'm praying with all my heart that there is really someone up there . . . someplace . . . so maybe, maybe . . . I'll get to see Jenny and Noah again."

There was a night that autumn, a few days after school began, when Dan and Molly finished dinner. He picked up the dishes, and Molly loaded them into the dishwasher. Afterward, they sat on the porch in the night still fragrant with the scents of summer, watching the lingering streamers of a scarlet and purple sunset fade into the blackness of the horizon. He knew they were both thinking of Noah.

Around them in the houses of the small town, people were finishing dinner, picking up and washing their dishes, some drawn to their porches, watching the descent of night as he and Molly were watching it then.

He felt the wind rising and heard the sound of a bough scraping across the roof above the porch. A shadowed figure passed on the walk before the house, a neighbor holding a dog pulling at its leash. From some house farther up the street, the wind carried the plaintive crying of a child. A car passed, for an instant the yellow beams from the headlights sweeping the porch and their figures sitting in their chairs. Afterward, the velvet dark of night returned.

A little later, the moon emerged, a yellowish glow that presaged the arrival of autumn. The stars appeared, a misty honeycomb of light that brightened and became visible to the naked eye. Dan recalled the hours he had spent with Noah, peering into the vastness of the sky. He remembered his son's excitement as Noah discovered the bright stars Castor and Pollux in the constellation of the Gemini. Hugging the southern horizon, part of the Milky Way, were the constellations of Sagittarius the Archer and Scorpius the Scorpion. Above them all was Antares, Scorpio's brightest star, a red supergiant that rivaled Mars. All that knowledge of space Dan had gained from his son.

Now he considered the stars and constellations that had shone throughout the existence of their small planet, glittering above fiery conflagrations and torrential rains, over fossils frozen in Ice Age glaciers, across the crumbled columns of vanquished kingdoms and lost civilizations, over the bleached bones of emperors and kings.

In the majesty of the eternal, expanding universe with its comets and its constellations, their own planet, home to weak creatures of flesh, blood, and bone, mortals unsubstantial as shadows, wingless, fleeting and dreamlike, given to senseless slaughters and to futile wars, humans might appear no more significant than the fireflies that speckled the night. Yet the marvel was that in all the endless vault of space, it was on their fragile planet, Earth, that love had been born. It was the love that drew two people together, that welcomed a newborn into life, that nourished and raised a child, that mended the torn edges of sorrow, and, finally, a love that redeemed humans from the finality of their death. To have shared such a love with Molly and to have had their love conceive and embrace the jewel of Noah for even the brief span of his life was a matchless bounty. Was it so remote a hope that somewhere, such love—so powerful that it overshadowed the majesty of the sovereign planets—that such love, once separated, might again be reunited?

In that instant of divination, he embraced the closeness of his son, a proximity of such substance that he felt if he shut his eyes and reached out his hand he might touch Noah's hand.

He heard Molly sigh, and in a strange prescience knew that her thoughts were the same as his own. The memories of their dead son had carried the power of the revelation to both of them, a vision of some indefinable and haunting beauty, born on the waves of night.

After a while they rose, still without feeling any need to speak, and entered the house to go to bed.

HARRY MARK PETRAKIS is the author of twenty previous books, including novels, memoirs, and collections of short stories and essays. He has twice been nominated for the National Book Award in Fiction, and his work has appeared in the *Atlantic Monthly, Harper's Bazaar, Playboy, Mademoiselle,* the *Chicago Tribune,* and the *New York Times.* In 1992, he held the Kazantzakis Chair in Modern Greek Studies at San Francisco State University. For the past forty years, he has also been a lecturer and storyteller, often reading his stories to college and club audiences in the old bardic tradition. He and his wife, Diana, live in the Indiana Dunes overlooking Lake Michigan. They have three sons and four grandchildren.